MANIAC ON THE LOOSE

As he drew closer, Clint caught a smell that made his hand drop down to the modified Colt at his side. It was a familiar smell that always reminded him of rust and copper.

It was blood.

He could smell it, and now that he was close enough, he could easily see that it was too thin to be paint and too red and thick to be much of anything else. It was blood alright. And now that he was less than a few paces away from the front door, he could hear a muffled *thump,* which was only too familiar.

Gunfire.

Clint didn't bother with the steps. Instead, he launched himself up when he reached the boardwalk and landed directly to one side of the door. He kept moving to avoid the window, turning on the ball of his foot until he could press his back against the wall beside the painted glass panes.

He didn't waste another second before taking a quick glance through the window. What he saw was along the lines of an execution. Maybe even a full-fledged massacre.

DON'T MISS THESE
ALL-ACTION WESTERN SERIES
FROM THE BERKLEY PUBLISHING GROUP

THE GUNSMITH by J. R. Roberts
  Clint Adams was a legend among lawmen, outlaws, and ladies.
  They called him . . . the Gunsmith.

LONGARM by Tabor Evans
  The popular long-running series about Deputy U.S. Marshal
  Long—his life, his loves, his fight for justice.

SLOCUM by Jake Logan
  Today's longest-running action Western. John Slocum rides
  a deadly trail of hot blood and cold steel.

BUSHWHACKERS by B. J. Lanagan
  An action-packed series by the creators of Longarm! The
  rousing adventures of the most brutal gang of cutthroats ever
  assembled—Quantrill's Raiders.

DIAMONDBACK by Guy Brewer
  Dex Yancey is Diamondback, a Southern gentleman turned
  con man when his brother cheats him out of the family for-
  tune. Ladies love him. Gamblers hate him. But nobody pulls
  one over on Dex . . .

WILDGUN by Jack Hanson
  The blazing adventures of mountain man Will Barlow—from
  the creators of Longarm!

TEXAS TRACKER by Tom Calhoun
  Meet J. T. Law: the most relentless—and dangerous—
  manhunter in all Texas. Where sheriffs and posses fail, he's
  the best man to bring in the most vicious outlaws—for a
  price.

THE GUNSMITH

259

A KILLER'S HANDS

J. R. ROBERTS

JOVE BOOKS, NEW YORK

A KILLER'S HANDS

A Jove Book / published by arrangement with
the author

PRINTING HISTORY
Jove edition / July 2003

ISBN: 0-515-13578-X

A JOVE BOOK®
Jove Books are published by The Berkley Publishing Group,
a division of Penguin Group (USA) Inc.,
375 Hudson Street, New York, New York 10014.
JOVE and the "J" design
are trademarks belonging to Penguin Group (USA) Inc.

PRINTED IN THE UNITED STATES OF AMERICA

10 9 8 7 6 5 4 3 2 1

ONE

"I'm glad you came in to see me," the doctor said as he stared into the eyes of his newest patient and snapped his fingers in front of the other man's face. Noting the patient's response to the noise and movement, he nodded and kept on talking. "By the looks of it, I'd say you were overdue for a visit quite a while ago."

The man sat on the long, narrow bed toward the back of the doctor's office, his hands resting on his lap, his back slightly stooped. His long legs hung over the side enough for the bottoms of his feet to touch the floor. He allowed himself to blink at the doctor's snapping and let out a long, impatient breath.

"Am I right?" the doctor asked. Judging by his body alone, the doctor might have been mistaken for a farmhand or some other kind of laborer. His arms were thick and muscular, his torso barrel-shaped and solid. As he waited for a response to his question, the doctor fixed his keen brown eyes on the patient and let a stern expression come over him.

The patient looked back into those eyes, picking up immediately on the intelligence in them. Finally, after waiting a few more seconds didn't force the doctor to move along with his examination, the man said, "Yeah. You're right."

"I certainly am, Mr. Darrow. I can tell by the color of your skin and these bloodshot eyes that your condition is advanced."

When the patient laughed, his sunken cheeks looked as though they rested directly against his skull, the smile curling the corners of his mouth upward from their normal, drooping position. He didn't look as bad as some of the patients who had come through the doctor's office. In fact, apart from the near-skeletal look of his face and the pasty color of his skin, the patient seemed to be doing rather well.

Actually, he seemed to be doing rather well in spite of those things. When the patient moved, he did so with smooth precision, as though he was consciously measuring every last motion. The motions were strong, however, and his body showed no hint of weakness apart from the appearance of its outer shell.

"What symptoms have you been experiencing, Mr. Darrow?"

After another sigh, Darrow said, "I'm feeling better, so why don't I save us both some trouble and get out of here?"

Hearing that, the doctor leaned back in his chair and turned to look at the woman who'd been standing silently in the back of his office. Her hair was as black as a raven's wing and was tied off to one side by a thin black ribbon. Her skin was almost as pale as Darrow's, but with a more pearly sheen to it. Obviously, her pallor came from lack of sun rather than anything that might be ailing her. Until that point, she might as well have been a part of the wall since she hadn't made a noise or moved a muscle.

She started moving just then, however, and didn't need to see the exasperated look on the physician's face. "You're already here, Ellis," she said to the man sitting on the doctor's bed. "Just tell Doctor Laird what's wrong and maybe he can help you."

"We're here because you made me come here," Darrow snapped. When he raised his voice, it took on a raspy edge that sounded just as painful as it felt. "And if he can help me, he should be working somewhere else besides this piss hole of a town in the middle of nowhere!"

The woman wanted to say something by way of a reply, but pursed her lips tightly together instead to keep the words from slipping out. Her dark eyes smoldered for a second before she looked away, crossed her arms over her chest, and turned to face the wall behind her.

"She's only got your best interests at heart," Doctor Laird said.

When Darrow shifted his gaze from the woman to the doctor, Laird got the sudden urge to look away as well. "Really?" Darrow said. "And what the hell do you know about it?"

"I may not know your personal business, but I can tell that you're a sick man and that you need to stay here for a couple of days. She was right to bring you here. Obviously you didn't want to come in on your own, but if you didn't, you might not have made it much longer."

Although he didn't seem as stricken as might have been expected at hearing this news, Darrow let his anger fade away and he nodded slowly.

Taking any opportunity he could get to address his patient, Doctor Laird continued, "Have you been short of breath recently?"

Darrow nodded.

"Do you get the shakes and feel weak sometimes?"

Obviously bristling at the very notion that he might be considered weak, Darrow clenched his teeth together and wrapped his fingers tightly around the edge of the bed. Even with that tension going through him, he still nodded.

"And when was the last time you've seen a doctor about this matter?"

Darrow looked down, as though he was searching for an answer on the tops of his boots and the backs of his hands. When he spoke next, his pale lips parted, but his teeth remained locked together. "Three weeks ago."

From across the room, the dark-haired woman cleared her throat and fixed Darrow with an intense stare.

"Maybe closer to five weeks," Darrow corrected himself. "Or even six."

Darrow could feel the scolding that was about to come spilling out of the doctor at any second. He'd heard it several times before from several other doctors, but that didn't make it any easier to bear. It was bad enough that he felt like his body was falling apart; the last thing Darrow wanted to hear was a tongue-lashing for trying to live while he still had the chance.

But even though Dr. Laird's face betrayed his true feelings, he somehow managed to keep himself from saying a word. Instead, he shook his head almost imperceptibly and placed his hands on either side of Darrow's neck. "Does this hurt?" he asked, while pressing in slightly.

Darrow winced and said, "A little."

"Take a deep breath and hold it."

When he followed through with that order, Darrow sounded like he was trying to suck air through a wet, broken pipe. The pain that was already attacking him doubled once his lungs were almost full, but he held the breath anyway, choking back the pain as though it was a contest.

"Now let it out." Dr. Laird's eyes narrowed as he paid close attention to what he heard and felt when his patient emptied his lungs. "I don't have to tell you that waiting so long to see me was a big mistake. In fact, traveling at all isn't a good idea. Where do you hail from, anyway?"

It was the woman who answered. "Saint Louis," she said.

"I hope you're not planning on leaving here anytime soon."

"No, we'll be staying for a—"

"We won't be staying long," Darrow interrupted. "Maybe just another day." When he saw the look on the woman's face, he snarled in the back of his throat and added, "Maybe another day or two."

She seemed satisfied by that, but not much.

"Where are you staying?" Laird asked.

Before she could be interrupted again, the woman said, "At that hotel right down the street. The big one with the fancy sign."

"I know the place. I'll come by there later tonight to check on you. In the meantime, I want you to drink plenty of hot liquids and top it off with some sweets."

"Sweets?" Darrow asked.

"That's right. The general store has some rock candy and taffy. If that's not to your liking, put extra sugar in your coffee or tea."

"And that's supposed to help?"

"I'll check on that when I see you again. Normally, I'd like to keep closer watch on you for a while, but since you don't plan on staying too long, I'll have to do what I can while you're here. I can check in on you on my way home tonight. Let's say around eight or nine."

"That would be great, Doctor," the woman said, even though Laird's tone hadn't implied that he would take any other response. "I'll make sure he's there."

"Good. Because if he's not there, I'll come looking for him. This may be a good-sized town, Mr. Darrow, but I know enough people to track you down without too much effort."

Traces of exasperation were still evident on Darrow's

face, but he managed to keep himself from sighing heavily. "Fine, fine," he said by way of surrendering. "I'll be there."

With that, Darrow got up from the bed and picked his jacket up from where it had been lying beside him. As he moved to slip into the jacket, the twin holsters hanging beneath his arms could easily be seen. Until that moment, he'd been keeping the weapons covered as much as he could. The holsters had been peeking out the entire time and Dr. Laird hadn't once asked for them to be removed.

Once he got his jacket on, Darrow straightened up to his full height and extended a pasty, sweaty hand. "Thanks, Doc. I appreciate your time."

Darrow's handshake was strong, but the doctor's was firm enough to match it. "Just try to heed my words, Ellis, or you won't have much time."

Looking straight into the doctor's eyes, Ellis Darrow let the muscles in his jaw relax and lifted his chin. From there, he simply nodded, took the woman by the hand and walked out of the office.

TWO

There were plenty of joys to be had in life.

Depending on what kind of a man was making the list, the joys near the top could vary greatly. There was the joy of holding a gold nugget the size of a fist and there was the joy of opening a fresh bottle of imported Scotch. Some men preferred music or art and others took their pleasure from having friends and relatives close by.

Although all of those things were fine and good, Clint Adams was having a good enough time indulging in some of the simpler pleasures of life. At the moment, he enjoyed the fact that his belly was full, the breeze was cool and the beer in his hand was even cooler.

Sitting in a sturdy chair outside a quiet restaurant on Mill Street, Clint had one foot crossed over the other, propped upon the rail at the edge of the boardwalk. He could feel the warm dinner working its way through his system, urged on by the occasional sip of a surprisingly well-brewed beer.

When he'd first gotten back to that part of the country, Clint had made what he'd thought was a small mistake at the time. A letter had been forwarded to him from Labyrinth, Texas, by his friend Rick Hartman, who owned a saloon down there. The letter was from a woman that Clint had known a little while ago.

Her name was Maribeth Tweed and she was working her way through Montana as a singer. She went from town to town and stage to stage, looking for a place that seemed good enough for her to settle. Despite its unfortunate name, Broken Cross, Montana was just such a place. At least, became such a place once Clint lent his hand to the local sheriff in routing out a group of thugs who'd chosen to settle there as well.

The thugs turned out to be a bunch of dogs who ran away with their tails between their legs when they realized who it was that had thrown in on the side of the law. All Clint had to do was show his face and tell them to leave and the gunmen were only too happy to oblige.

It wasn't a very exciting story, but it had a happy enough ending. Once the bad element had been weeded out, Broken Cross became a much more inviting place in the eyes of everyone from gamblers to investors. In the saloon trade, many times those two groups tended to share members equally.

According to the letter Clint had received, Maribeth had sunk all of her earnings into a saloon and had eventually gotten the place built up to one of the finest in Broken Cross. Clint and Maribeth had parted on good terms and since she'd heard about him showing up on her side of the country, she decided to try her luck and invite him to come her way. Out of courtesy—and a lack of things to do on the particular night he'd received the letter—Clint had written her back and agreed to meet her when he got the chance.

Being the person she was, Maribeth took that as a full acceptance to her invitation and even set the time for Clint to arrive. He knew her well enough to be certain that she would hold on to that notion like a dog with its teeth sunk into a pork steak and it would be better to make an appearance while he was still less than a day or two's ride away. Besides, all of the memories he had of Maribeth were good ones and there really wasn't any reason to disappoint her.

He'd ridden into town feeling that he was fulfilling an obligation that he could have ignored if he'd only tossed that letter away. But as soon as he set his eyes on the busty, full-figured woman who ran out of her saloon to meet him, Clint realized that ignoring that letter would have been a mistake.

The time they'd spent away from each other hadn't been kind to Maribeth. Actually, that time had downright spoiled her rotten. No longer dancing for a living, Maribeth had lost her lean, tightly muscular build and had taken on a softer, rounder appearance. Her hips were smooth and contoured. Her face was warm and pleasant. Her breasts even seemed to bounce more as she dashed outside with her arms held open wide.

"Clint Adams, as I live and breathe!" she said. "You sure didn't waste any time getting here!"

"Why would I waste any time? I said I'd be here didn't I?"

"Well I didn't expect you to drop everything and make a race out of it. I was half-thinking you wouldn't take me up on my invitation at all."

Clint swept her up into his arms and lifted her off her feet. She still felt like a dancer as she hopped up and rested her hands on his shoulders while allowing herself to be spun around. Her smile was just as he remembered and her body was firm and solid beneath his hands.

"You're looking good, Maribeth," Clint said without trying to disguise the desire that crept into his voice.

"Aw, you don't have to say that. I know I'm not the wisp of a girl I was when you left town."

"No, you're not." Pulling her tightly against him, Clint leaned down and let his lips drift over the side of her neck, just the way he knew she liked it. "You're better." He kissed her gently there and worked his way up to her ear. When he whispered to her, he could feel her tremble slightly in his grasp. "If I'd have known you were looking this good, I might have made a race of it after all."

Her lightly tanned skin turned a little redder when she felt Clint's hands wander down her back to pat her on her backside. She let her teeth drift over her luscious bottom lip when she smiled and reached around to slap Clint's rump in kind.

"Is that why you came back to see me?" she asked in a voice tinted with overly dramatic disappointment. "Did you just come here to bed me and leave?"

Clint let his eyes roll up into his head as though he was seriously thinking over his answer. "Well, now that you mention it, that did have something to do with it."

Maintaining her hurt expression for all of two more seconds, Maribeth broke out in a naughty grin and leaned forward to playfully bite Clint's lip. "Good," she said after her quick nibble. "Because this town's chock full of puritans and a woman's got her own needs."

"That's the Maribeth I remember. Are you still as good a cook as you were?"

"Yep. And that's why I intend to have one of the people working for me make your supper. I can't have you keeling over from food poisoning before I get my hands on you."

"Oh, so you plan on making me wait through supper?"

Once again, she put on a pouting expression. "A girl's got to play hard to get. Besides, you're going to need your strength."

THREE

The place Maribeth took Clint to was not the saloon where she had a controlling interest. It was actually a place in a quieter part of town that seemed to cater to the more up-standing crowd than the type that frequented her saloon. Remembering the one sample Clint had had of her cooking, he was praying that she would know he was kidding when he asked if she was going to fix supper herself.

Not only did Maribeth not like to cook, but she was astonishingly bad at it. The first morning they'd spent together, she'd tried to fry up some eggs and brown some bacon. What he'd gotten was a runny mess and some charred strips of leather on a plate.

Needless to say, she took no offense at Clint's comments then or later when they'd met up again. Apparently, she had bought a small piece of the restaurant as a backup in case something happened to her saloon. It was a smart business plan and a damn good place to eat.

Clint ordered steak, peas, and corn bread and his only regret was that he couldn't fit any more of the wonderful meal into his stomach. Every bite melted in his mouth and the beer that was served washed it down perfectly. Maribeth sat with him for as long as she could before having to go back and tend to some matters at her saloon.

Once he was finished with his meal, Clint was able to waddle outside, drop himself into a chair and lift his feet up onto the rail along the edge of the boardwalk. The summer was slowly losing its edge and the sunset brought with it a cool, refreshing breeze. He took the next couple minutes to savor the simple pleasures of life and sip the last few drops of his beer.

Clint smiled when he thought that he'd actually considered skipping by this place and writing some flimsy excuse to Maribeth. Right off hand, he couldn't even remember why he might have done such a thing. All that he cared about anymore was that he was glad he hadn't. Broken Cross was a good place to kick back and let a few good days roll over him.

As the last bit of his beer dribbled down his throat, Clint took a moment to soak everything in. The restaurant was called Jesse's. Clint only found that out when he craned his neck around to look at the little sign hanging from a set of hooks next to the door. It seemed as though Jesse's was the only thing open on that stretch of street as far as he could see.

There was a couple stores nearby and a doctor's office, but none of those seemed to be doing any business at the moment. There were a few people strolling down the street and most of those appeared to be taking in the dusk just as leisurely as Clint. They talked quietly among themselves and headed their own directions.

Suddenly, the calm was jostled as the door to the doctor's office came open and a couple stepped outside. Although they seemed to be in a hurry and spoke in quick, sharp tones, they weren't being loud enough for Clint to overhear what they were saying. Instead, they disrupted the scene in front of him much the way a pebble disrupts a still pond.

Everything around him had seemed so still that Clint

had almost thought of the street as a painting for him to take in and admire. His thoughts were just as relaxed as his body, and when those two walked through that door, it was as if someone had just stepped through his painting.

Clint's eyes were on the couple when he heard another sound approaching from behind. That sound was footsteps treading lightly on the floorboards and coming at him from the restaurant door, which had been propped open by a ceramic jug. A casual glance over his shoulder confirmed his suspicions and he turned his attention back to the street.

"So how was dinner?" Maribeth asked as she stepped up behind him and began rubbing his shoulders.

"I think if you brought more business to be fed by that cook of yours, you'd be a rich woman in no time at all."

"I'll have to think that over. Is there any chance you might be looking for an investment opportunity?"

"Aww, don't tell me that's why you invited me here. And I was just starting to relax."

Clint could feel one of her hands move away and then there came the gentle brush of Maribeth's hair against the side of his face. She leaned in close to him and let her breath warm his ear.

"I don't need investors, Mr. Adams. I just like being kind to them that was kind to me." After saying that, she let her tongue flick out just enough to touch the tip against his earlobe. "And it's refreshing to see a man who isn't so damned full of himself."

"I take it that last comment was sarcastic?"

"Oh yeah. Couldn't you tell?"

Clint smiled and shook his head. "I could tell. Sorry if I stepped out of line, there."

"No problem. Here," Maribeth said while reaching around to slip the tip of a thin cigar between his lips. "I thought you might like this after your meal."

Normally, Clint wasn't much of a smoker. But before

he could protest, Maribeth had already struck a match and lit the cigar she'd given him. As soon as its end started to burn, a smooth rich flavor drifted into his mouth and swirled around before floating back over his lips.

"Damn," Clint said after puffing slightly. "You sure know how to treat your guests."

"Sure I do. And if I treated them all like this, I probably would be a rich woman." Saying that, Maribeth stepped around Clint's chair and settled into his lap. "I've been thinking about you ever since I found that address in Labyrinth. And when I actually heard back from you, I started planning all the different ways I could thank you for all you did for me."

Clint ran his hands along her body, feeling the firm curves of her hips and waist. "It wasn't much. Actually, if one of the deputies said they were me I might not have even had to be here."

"That little mess with them two-bit cowboys is not what I'm talking about, Clint. I'm talking about you treating me like a woman instead of a whore. You made me see I could be strong enough to follow through on my dreams. If it wasn't for you, I'd still be dancing in a saloon instead of running one."

For a moment, they both just looked into the other's eyes, saying things they didn't even need words to say.

Finally, Clint gave her a gentle kiss on the lips. "I wonder what would have happened if there was any shooting."

"If there was a lot of shooting, you never would have gotten a chance to tell me that I could do anything I set my mind to. Do you remember that talk?"

As soon as she mentioned it, that conversation sprung into Clint's mind as though it had happened yesterday. "Yes. I do."

"I'll never forget it. You might not have thought much of it, but you were the first man who didn't laugh when I told him about all the things I wanted to do and all the ambitions I had. That meant a lot to me, Clint. It still does. That was all I needed to get me to where I am today. Nobody else would even give me that much, but you did and that says a lot about what kind of man you are."

"Well, it was my pleasure," Clint replied.

Getting up, Maribeth took Clint's hand and pulled him to his feet. "Follow me to my room. Then I'll show you what your pleasure is."

Laughing softly as he allowed himself to be led away, Clint whispered, "What was that you were saying about being treated like a whore?"

"There's a time and a place for everything, my good man. The place is only a few streets away."

"And the time?"

"As soon as we get there."

FOUR

Whenever Ellis Darrow walked through a door, his eyes darted back and forth as if they were twitching nervously in their sockets. Every time his surroundings changed, his first instinct was to take in every last detail before he had a chance to be surprised. It was a predator's instinct of surveying the hunting ground before he stepped foot upon new ground. To the outside world, however, it was just another thing in a long line of things that made him look different from nearly everyone else around him.

Ellis Darrow didn't mind being different. He'd been different his entire life and he'd come to enjoy the effect his eccentricities had upon the so-called "normal" folks. With enough practice, he'd found a way to make his oddities work in his favor. And after thirty-two years of practice, he had more advantages than any normal man could ever ask for. Of course, he would have traded all of those advantages for one thing that the rest of the world seemed to have which he most certainly did not: a fighting chance at surviving to see the next sunrise.

"That doctor was feeding me what I wanted to hear," Ellis said as he and the raven-haired woman walked out of Laird's office.

"How can you say that?"

"Jesus Christ, Ann, you've been with me long enough to spot a phony when you see one. You've spent enough time with me to know that he left out one particular detail when he was spouting off that prognosis back there."

Ann stopped and crossed her arms over her chest. Cocking her hip to one side, she fixed him with a stern gaze and said, "He also told you something that you never heard before. Are you forgetting that?"

"What? About the sweets? Yeah, there's a real headline. That just might cure the burning in my skin or the pain when I breathe. I'm dying, Ann, there ain't no amount of taffy or sugar in my tea that's gonna change that."

Although she tried to maintain the toughness in her face, Ann was unable to keep the tears from forming in the corners of her eyes. "I hate to hear you talk like that. You know I do."

"Then don't listen. If you can't tell I'm dying just by looking at me, then you need to see a doctor yourself. If you can't face facts, then I don't need you around, anyway." He stopped just after stepping into the street and straightened his posture until he looked ramrod straight.

His hawk's eyes swept the street and surrounding boardwalks. As far as he could tell, there weren't any people around who were interested in listening to what they were saying. Apart from that, there was a man sitting with his feet propped up on a rail, but he was soon distracted by an attractive woman who appeared from the restaurant behind him.

More and more, Darrow felt his back start to stoop if he didn't keep constant watch on his posture. It was just another instance of his body wanting to give up the constant struggle while his mind fought to go on.

"I hate when you talk to me like that," Ann said. "And after all I've been through with you, I can't believe you would have the nerve to talk to me like I'm some kind of nuisance."

After a long pause, Darrow said, "You know I don't think that. I'm sorry, Ann. It's just that I don't know how many more doctors I can take."

"But this one seemed nice enough. And he found things that you never even told him about. Not even the other doctors we've seen have guessed about the shakes and the dizzy spells."

"That's because those just started up."

"Yeah. A month or two ago."

This time, when Darrow sighed it sounded more exhausted than exasperated. "You're right. Maybe I should see him later tonight after all. That means that we'll have to hold off on those other things we were planning on doing."

"I figured that much." She smiled and hooked her arm through his. "I think it's funny."

"What's funny?"

"That you were so sure I was going to let you be anywhere else besides in that hotel waiting for that doctor to see you. After all, he's the main reason we came to this town."

"For you, maybe. I had another reason for being here."

"Right. But, like you said, that's going to have to wait."

Once again, the couple started walking down the street. Darrow looked over to the man who'd been sitting on the boardwalk and he seemed plenty occupied by the woman who was now sitting on his lap. Both of them got up and started walking down the boardwalk as well, keeping their backs to Darrow and Ann.

He wasn't quite sure what it was, but Darrow got a strange feeling when he looked at that other man. It was the odd, instinctive ringing in his ears that a man got when he saw a familiar face from a long time ago or heard a song that he just couldn't quite name. The more he thought about it, the more that feeling itched in the back of his skull like a gnat buzzing around while looking for a way outside.

"What's the matter?" Ann asked.

Darrow shook his head and turned to look at her. "It's nothing. I just thought I might have seen that man up there before."

She didn't make a big show of it, but Ann glanced toward the other couple as well, studying them without being obvious about it to any of the few others passing by. After a matter of seconds, she shrugged and looked up at him. "I can't see him well enough to say anything. Do you think he may be trouble?"

"I don't know yet."

"Should we check on him just to make sure?"

"No," Darrow answered after a few moments' consideration. "Not yet, anyway. I'd like to get some time in at the card tables before you send me to my room."

"And what about the rest of our business?"

"That's still on schedule. Just be sure you take your walk tonight and let me know what you find."

"I will."

The rest of the time it took for them to stroll to their hotel was passed in silence. It wasn't the awkward kind of silence, however. In fact, it was much the opposite. The quiet that settled in between them felt more like a warm, comfortable quilt that had covered them both for many a cold night.

Their arms were entwined tightly and every step seemed to bring them closer together. Before too long, Ann rested her head on Darrow's shoulder and let out a contented sigh that always reminded Darrow of the way a cat purrs just before it falls asleep.

At moments like those, Darrow felt more alive than any other time. That was when the pain from his many ailments didn't quite sting so badly. It was then that his aching muscles and organs went numb, which was a hell of a lot better than the constant straining agony that they usually gave to him along with every breath and beat of his heart.

He could feel the blood pumping through him just a little quicker and when that happened, it allowed him to either forget the pain or channel it into something else that was much more useful: energy. Like a swimmer who'd somehow managed to get behind an oncoming wave, Darrow rode his pain throughout its constant crests and pushed himself farther than most healthy men could go.

"I love you, Ann," he said softly.

She smiled and nestled her head against him. "I know."

FIVE

The Tweed House wasn't the biggest saloon in town, but it was easily one of the most popular. For a town the size of Broken Cross, there was plenty of business to be had for any good saloon owner and for one as ambitious as Maribeth Tweed, the business was easier to take than a fat apple hanging at the end of a branch.

With a little attention paid to the gamblers who made their way around the country, word of mouth had spread about the place, giving it the kind of advertisement that money simply couldn't buy. Using her own knowledge and a few favors called in from her days as a dancer, Maribeth also managed to fill the stage with quality entertainment to draw in the crowds that weren't normally attracted to places like saloons.

When Clint was led back to The Tweed House, he barely recognized the place. "Was this even here the last time I was in town?" he asked as he recovered from the shock of seeing the large, finely decorated building.

"It was, but it wasn't anything like this. I used nearly all my savings to build this place up. It cost me triple the amount I needed to buy my share of the holdings to begin with. You should see my partner's face when he thinks about it. I swear his veins pop every time."

"I could understand why. Hell, I'm not even in the saloon business and I wish I had thrown in when I had the chance."

The inside was split down the middle into two distinct parts. On one side was a section of card tables and a bar set up in the back corner of the room. The bar made its corner into a square, giving the tenders plenty of space to walk back and forth between shelves of liquor bottles. The other part of the room was taken up by a large stage, complete with a spotlight in the rafters and a thick, red, velvety curtain.

Following his line of sight, Maribeth said, "I probably spent more than I should have on that stage, but I couldn't help myself. Besides, I may know lots of the country's best acts on a first-name basis, but they won't perform just any old place."

"A few big shows should make it worth your while, huh?"

"Actually, they already have." She lowered her voice to a whisper and leaned in a little closer. "I've paid for that expensive curtain several times over, but I don't tell my partner that. It makes Jasper feel better if he thinks I'm still in debt to someone."

Before Clint could ask why she was whispering, a fat man with several sets of chins instead of a neck waddled up and slapped a fake smile onto his blubbery face. "And who do we have here?" the fat man asked. "A friend of yours? Someone else to drink for free?"

Smiling even wider than the fat man, yet still making it look sincere, Maribeth said, "Jasper, I'd like you to meet an old friend of mine. This is Clint Adams. He's visiting for a few days."

"Clint Adams? I . . . uhhh . . . didn't mean to be rude, but I was just . . ."

"Just making an ass out of yourself as always," Maribeth finished, while still displaying her winning smile. "And before you say another word, I do believe his drinks will be on the house."

Jasper blustered and turned a shade of red that was even darker than the stage's expensive curtain. "Oh of course, of course. After what he did for Broken Cross, I wouldn't have it any other way." He threw his hand out like a walrus offering up its flipper. "Pleased to meet you, Mr. Adams. Enjoy your stay."

Clint shook the fat man's hand and nodded politely. Jasper's grip was wet and loose, sending an uncomfortable itch down Clint's back. Thankfully, the handshake was cut off quickly as Jasper found some urgent business that required his attention in another part of the room.

"Charming fellow," Clint said while wiping his hand on the side of his leg.

"Only if you're his wife. She seems to be the only person in town who wouldn't rather slap him silly than say hello. Come on," Maribeth said while tugging on Clint's hand and leading him through the room. "I've got some better sights to show you."

They were halfway through the saloon when the lights on the stage section of the room started to dim. There was a rattle of movement as someone crawled out onto the rafters via a narrow path made out of planks suspended from the ceiling. Once at the end of the planks, the small figure settled in behind the spotlight and brought it blazing to life.

No sooner had the light hit the curtain than the velvet barrier was pulled in half and gathered up on either side of the stage. Not only was a large, polished stage revealed, but a small orchestra pit as well. The musicians there struck up their instruments and launched directly into a lively melody as a pair of women sauntered into the light.

"I'll be damned," Clint said as he let himself be pulled along by his guide. "You really did go all out!"

"I told you. Only the best."

They were at the back of the room by now and getting closer to the bar, which was already starting to get crowded. Maribeth fished a key from a pocket in her skirt and unlocked a door marked PRIVATE. From there, she all but shoved Clint inside and then stepped in herself.

Closing the door behind her, she turned the latch and fixed Clint with a hungry, leering stare. "Finally, I've got you all to myself."

Clint stepped up to her and placed both hands against the door, one on either side of her head. He didn't allow her to move so much as an inch as he slowly pressed his body against hers and moved his hands down along the smooth curve of her neck. He let his fingertips trace along her skin and listened to the way her breath shuddered as he drifted in to kiss her in the spot he'd just touched.

"So where are you taking me now?" he asked.

The only answer she gave was a glance over his shoulder. When Clint turned to look that way, he saw that they were standing at one end of a narrow hallway which branched out and ended at two separate doors.

"Is this the time and place you were telling me about?"

"Close," she said. "If you can stand to wait for just a little while longer, I can get us to the place I was referring to."

Clint shook his head. "That won't do. I'm thinking that now's the time and this is the place."

When he pressed himself against her, Clint's body told Maribeth everything she needed to know. And when she felt the hardness between his legs brush against her, she immediately came around to his line of thinking.

SIX

Maribeth leaned back against the door, closing her eyes as Clint began kissing her on the neck and shoulders. As his lips moved along her collarbone, they started drifting down along the plunging neckline of her dress. Her skin was soft and tender there, as if every nerve inside of her had been eagerly awaiting his touch.

She let out a soft moan as Clint's hands roamed up along her sides, starting at her hips and moving to cup her breasts. Pulling in a sharp breath when his hands closed around her bosom, she wrapped both arms around him and held him tightly.

Clint felt lost within the sweet scent of her flesh as he allowed himself to taste and feel wherever his instincts led him. Although he'd experienced her the last time he was in town, she had changed in so many ways that she seemed like a different woman.

Physically, her body was softer and more pleasing to the touch. Her breasts seemed fuller and her hips were more rounded and solid. She had the full figure of a woman rather than the lean wispy shape of the dancer she'd once been. Clint savored all of these differences as he moved his hands all over her body. The sensory feast

25

was made even better when she began to wriggle and grind against him.

She'd changed in other ways as well. Before, she'd been passionate and wild when they were in their most intimate moments. Now, she seemed more anxious to take him inside of her. Maribeth was more expressive and free with her passions, clawing at him and letting him know how much she enjoyed every last touch.

Grasping him tightly, she lifted one leg and wrapped it around his waist, letting out a slow moan as Clint reached down to hike up her skirt. Once the layers of material were out of his way, he slid his hand along the muscle of her thigh until he got to the smoother, softer flesh between her legs.

Maribeth's eyes snapped open and she let out a surprised groan when Clint moved his fingers over her panties. He could feel that she was already moist for him and Clint used the expressions on her face as a guide to tell him where to touch her next. His eyes locked on to hers as his hand moved beneath her skirt until finally he found the spot that tensed every one of Maribeth's muscles.

Clint's other hand snaked around her back to hold her in place and he leaned forward so that his mouth was less than an inch from her cheek.

"Oh, God, Clint," she whispered. "I've been thinking about this for so long."

He didn't answer. He didn't have to. Clint let his actions speak for him as he hooked his fingers around the side of her panties and closed his fist over the flimsy material. With a quick yank, he tore the undergarment off of her and threw it to the floor.

Her back straightening at the sound of the ripping material, Maribeth smiled widely and playfully smacked Clint on the shoulder. "Those were expensive, you know. I think they were imported from Paris."

"Really? Then you'll just have to teach me a lesson."

Maribeth looked at him as though she was just about to step up to a challenge. After dropping her foot back down to the floor, she used both hands to push Clint away.

He allowed himself to be forced backward, but only for a step. Once he settled into his spot, he saw Maribeth reach down and start tugging at his belt. In no more than a second or two, the belt was off and his pants were unfastened. Despite everything else that was going on inside of him, Clint had to take a moment and pause to say, "Nice trick. I don't even think I could do that so fast."

"If you like that trick, then you're really going to enjoy the rest of what's in store for you."

Before Clint could say another word, he felt Maribeth's hands sliding down along his stomach, working their way to his erect penis. Her fingers curled around him and she started massaging him gently back and forth. She moved her hand faster until she could feel that she was the one making Clint start to tense in every muscle.

Just when she could tell he was about to reach down for her, she leaned forward, opened her mouth and closed her lips around the tip of his cock. Maribeth felt Clint's hands rest on her shoulders as she took him all the way inside, running her tongue up and down along the bottom of his shaft.

Clint wanted to lift her to her feet so he could satisfy his hunger to be inside of her, but wasn't about to stop her from what she was doing. Her mouth moved expertly over the length of him, sending waves of chills throughout his entire body.

She parted her lips slightly as she took him all the way inside her mouth, only to close them around the base of his cock, tightening them as she moved her head back and forth. Clint's fingers were sliding through her hair, holding her head in place when she reached the best spots and guiding her on to the next ones.

Only when she was ready did Maribeth get back to her

feet. Her eyes were smoldering with the heat of passion and the corners of her mouth curled up in a wicked smile.

For the next few moments, they stood there looking at each other and savoring the sexual tension crackling between them. The air seemed to warm and sting them all at once until finally neither one could hold themselves back any longer.

Clint was the first one to move and he surged forward to take her into his arms and lift her completely off her feet. Maribeth gave a little hop at the last second, wrapping both legs around him and grunting slightly when she felt her back bump against the wall.

After a few shifts of their bodies and a slight readjustment of her skirt, Clint felt his rigid cock sliding inside of her. Both of them let out satisfied moans as he drove forward and plunged himself in as far as he could go.

Only then could they both take a breath and once they did, they were once again lost in the sensations that overtook them as Clint began pumping in and out of her with a strong, solid rhythm.

SEVEN

Jasper didn't take a moment to look behind him until he was clear on the other side of the saloon. He made his rounds by waving to all the regulars and slapping the occasional back as though he was entertaining a royal court. In actuality, he was getting only half-hearted responses from his overly enthusiastic greetings and kicking up more dust than good feelings whenever his palm slapped against some cowboy's back.

Although many of the drinkers and card players asked him about his unusually good mood, Jasper didn't give any of them an answer. He just kept on moving until he found another hand to shake or drink to refill. Finally, once he'd made his way to the bar and dropped a shot of whiskey down his throat, Jasper turned around and looked at the couple he'd left behind.

With the growing crowd, he'd almost lost sight of Maribeth and the man she'd introduced as Clint Adams. Just when his hopes were about to soar through the roof, however, he spotted the two walking slowly through the room and stopping to admire the elaborately decorated stage. The instant his eyes hit that curtain, Jasper could feel his hackles rising on the back of his neck.

That damn curtain cost more than he earned in a month. Hell, knowing the way Maribeth lied to him about everything, it probably cost more than two good months' worth of his salary. But not her salary. Oh, no. She made more than him because she'd been lucky enough to guess that the saloon could be built up into something that could actually turn a profit. She was the star of the show and she never missed an opportunity to let him hear about it.

"Former dancer," Jasper grunted into his empty shot glass. "Huh. Former whore is more like it."

"What was that, Mr. Prescott?"

The question startled the fat man enough that if there had been any whiskey in his glass, he would have spilled it all over his shirt. Not that he had any real reason to be nervous. Besides recognizing the voice, he knew damn well that the only people in The Tweed House that called him Mr. Prescott was the hired help.

Still, even the help talked to Maribeth a hell of a lot more than they talked to Jasper. And on better terms, to boot.

"Nothing." Jasper snorted as he set his glass down upon the bar. "I just said I . . . uh . . . wanted some more. That would be more like it." Jasper topped off his clumsy lie with a wide smile.

The bartender shrugged, filled up Jasper's glass and moved on.

The moment the other man's back was turned, Jasper let his face droop into its familiar scowl. "Arrogant little prick," he thought. He just knew that one was going to go and tell whatever he thought he'd heard to Maribeth the moment he got a chance. Fortunately, the little prick wasn't going to have much of a chance.

With that thought in mind, Jasper felt a genuine smile coming on. He let it twist his blubbery lips into a comical expression, which, in his mind at least, must have been at least somewhat dashing. The smile disappeared once he leaned his back against the bar and his eyes were drawn back to the stage.

The lights were going dim, the spotlight was coming on and . . .

The spotlight. Another goddamn extravagance that had taken a cut out of what should have been Jasper's share of the profits. Maribeth had justified that just as she had that goddamn curtain, saying that it was things like that which would put The Tweed House on the map.

They had put The Tweed House on the map alright. Those things also put Jasper Prescott straight into the poorhouse when he should have been living on a prime piece of land just like the spot Maribeth had picked out to build her new house.

Music was starting to play and by the time Jasper had shaken off his self-pity, he'd lost sight of where Maribeth had dragged Clint Adams off to.

Perhaps that was all for the better, since Jasper wasn't comfortable seeing that man around The Tweed House at all. In fact, the farther Maribeth took that one, the better. Every local who'd lived in Broken Cross for more than a couple months knew all about Clint Adams and what he'd done. And the locals who'd lived there for more than a year or two would probably recognize the famed Gunsmith on sight.

Not that Jasper wasn't grateful for what Adams had done. He, like every other local owed Adams and the sheriff a debt of gratitude for making the streets safe to walk again. But with the plans that Jasper had in mind, a man like Clint Adams was the absolute last thing he wanted to see walking around his saloon.

As much as he hated to admit it, Jasper was starting to think that he should track down Maribeth just so he could find out what she'd done with her gun-toting friend.

No, he decided. There was no need for that. As long as Adams was somewhere out of sight, that should be just fine. The plan was set to go, all his players were falling into place, and if things went right, no one would be the wiser until Jasper was safely out of town and several states away.

The sloppy smile came back onto the fat man's face as he lifted his full glass of liquor up to his lips. He downed the fire water and felt a wave of heat pass through his system. His vision blurred ever so slightly, making him stop to count how many shot glasses he'd emptied in the last hour. Before he could nail down a specific number, Jasper spotted what he thought was a familiar figure making his way to the front door of the saloon.

"Ahhh." He sighed once he'd convinced himself that the man he'd just seen leaving the saloon was in fact Clint Adams. "Looks like my luck's holding up after all."

Suddenly, Jasper felt as though some of the weight of the world had been lifted from his shoulders. The heaviness that remained was the considerable weight of his own body, but he'd gotten used to waddling around with that some time ago.

He figured that the best place to find Maribeth was where she always went whenever she wasn't circulating around the saloon's main room. And now that he was sure Clint Adams had gone, Jasper wobbled over to the door marked PRIVATE and twisted the knob.

EIGHT

Clint moved his hips forward slowly, savoring the way his cock glided easily into Maribeth's body. Her moist lips took him in, surrounding him and clenching just a little when he drove all the way inside of her. With both hands cupping her firm backside, Clint could feel when she tensed. He lifted her up just a bit so that he could push into her again, just a little deeper than before.

Her fingernails dug into his back and shoulders as she felt herself being pushed against the door with every one of his thrusts. Just when she felt as though she was completely filled by him, Maribeth felt something move behind her.

"What was that?" Clint whispered.

She held her breath for a moment, feeling like a young girl who'd gotten caught by her father in the hayloft with a neighbor's son. "I don't know," she said.

They stepped apart from each other, but were still hesitant to take their hands off one another. Their clothes were a rumpled mess and they each looked as though they'd just come inside after running from one end of the town to another.

At that moment, the door rattled again. This time, however, the noise was followed by the distinct pounding of a fist against the door.

"Maribeth, are you in there?" came a muffled voice from the other side of the door.

Clint looked to her for an answer since he couldn't quite place the owner of the voice. It did sound familiar, but he wasn't entirely on his best game under the circumstances.

"It's Jasper," she said.

Rolling his eyes, Clint stepped forward and began moving his hands up and down Maribeth's body. "Let him wait," he whispered. "You've got more important business to tend to right now."

She squirmed against him, struggling to resist his advances, but not in a way that was anywhere close to being convincing. "Clint, I should really answer him. It may be—" The last bit of her words choked in her throat when Clint's hand slipped underneath her skirt and began gently rubbing the sensitive flesh between her legs.

If he wasn't already holding her, Clint felt that she might have stumbled when the chills coursed through her body. Maribeth slumped slightly in his arms, swooning from the pleasure that he was giving her with every brush of his fingers. The little show of her resisting him ended right there and she once again wrapped a leg around his waist while locking her fingers behind his neck. Clint pressed her up against a wall this time, where they could still hear the fat man testing the doorknob.

Her hands worked over his body as well, quickly coaxing him to a full erection in no time flat. Just as she was guiding him between her legs, the door rattled again, breaking their ability to block the rest of the world out for just another few moments.

"Dammit Maribeth, nobody else can get through here and I know you walked back there so let me in." Jasper was shouting so loudly that his voice echoed all the way down the short hallway. His pounding on the door was loud as well, reverberating through the enclosed space like a gunshot every time his hammy fist met wood.

"I might have to answer him," she said in between kissing Clint's neck and mouth. "He's persistent sometimes."

Clint grinned and moved his hips forward just enough for the tip of his penis to penetrate her flesh. "So am I."

Maribeth leaned her head back and let out a sigh that was slightly louder than she'd intended.

NINE

Standing outside the door, Jasper had his hand raised and was ready to start knocking yet again. That was when he heard what sounded like a sigh coming from just inside the private entrance. His mind raced with a couple different possibilities. First of all, he could just turn around and walk away from whatever was going on back there. Of course, that would mean putting off his plans for god only knew how long.

The second option was for him to just suck it up and take charge of the situation for a change. Before jumping to that kind of extreme, Jasper turned around and looked over the faces in the crowd one last time. Like a sign from above, he saw the front door open and a man step into the saloon. Not just any man, but the very man he'd been waiting for.

With renewed vigor, Jasper turned back toward the door and took hold of the handle. Now that he knew he had backup in case he happened to see Clint Adams standing next to Maribeth, Jasper fished a key from his pocket and fit it into the lock.

All it took was one twist of his wrist and the knob turned freely. Jasper opened the door and stepped inside

as though the fanfare coming from the nearby orchestra
was playing just for him.

"What the hell is—" Jasper started to say in a voice
that was filled with the bluster that he'd been building up
inside of him for the last couple of minutes. He stopped
talking, however, when he saw that there wasn't anyone
directly in front of him like he'd been expecting. In his
mind, he could still hear that sigh which sounded so close.
But there was no one directly in front of him. In fact,
Maribeth was at the other end of the hall.

Not only that, but she was alone.

"What's all the pounding about, Jasper?" Maribeth
asked while fussing with the front folds of her dress.

The fat man's eyes were still glancing around as though
he thought he might discover something that he hadn't
seen the first time he'd looked down the empty hallway.
"I . . . uhh . . . wanted to collect those documents and
make that deposit."

"You're going to the bank? Now?"

"Yeah, I arranged to have them stay open a little bit so
I didn't need to go in there with so many valuables. Are
you . . . alone?"

"Yes," Maribeth answered without so much as a twitch.
"Why?"

"What about Adams? Wasn't he with you?"

"He was, but I needed to come back here for a moment.
Did you try looking outside? After all, the show's starting
and everything. He's probably sitting out there close to
my stage." Maribeth knew damn well how much it irked
him when she mentioned anything to do with that expensive stage. And calling it "her stage" was just salt in the
wounds.

Jasper clenched everything he could clench and somehow forced himself to continue speaking before giving in
to the sudden compulsion he had to strangle the woman
in front of him. "Yeah. I guess I didn't look hard enough.

So what about those things I need? Could you get them out of the safe for me?"

Turning on her heel, Maribeth headed for the door on the right at the end of the hallway. It opened onto a small, yet comfortable office that was filled mostly by a rolltop desk and a few bookshelves. A small safe sat in the corner and she opened that while making sure she kept the combination shielded from Jasper's eyes.

Inside the safe was a bundle of papers tied together with twine and a burlap sack. She removed both of those things and handed them over to the fat man. Not bothering to close the safe, she escorted him to the door and down the hall.

"Are you sure you don't want an escort to the bank?" she asked. "I could have one of the boys walk with you just in case some—"

"I'll be fine," Jasper interrupted in a harsh tone. "Thanks all the same. You just get back to . . . whatever you were doing."

When Jasper opened the door leading back into the saloon, a wave of music and bawdy cheers came rolling in from the stage and audience gathered around it. With a tip of his hat, Jasper left. Maribeth shut the door and locked it behind him.

After waiting a few seconds, Maribeth turned and rushed down the hall. This time, once she reached the other end, she opened the door to the left and stepped through.

Behind that door was a staircase leading up to what had once been the building's attic. She hiked her skirt up a few inches, which allowed her to climb the stairs at something close to a run and reached another door at the top in no time at all. After rapping a few times upon the door, she opened it and hurried inside.

Clint was standing there, waiting in the middle of a lavishly decorated bedroom that would have been more at home inside a palace rather than atop a saloon. The walls were covered with dark paper and the floor was covered with a soft carpet. The few pieces of furniture were finely carved and polished and the bed in the middle of the room was fitted with a luxurious comforter.

Even the air inside the room smelled expensive, as it was flavored by the scent of candles and perfume. Clint hadn't moved from that spot since he'd stepped through the door a minute or so ago. He was still busy taking in all the extravagant details surrounding him.

"What the hell is this place?" Clint asked.

Maribeth smiled and walked up so she could wrap her arms around him. "This is my little hideaway. It's where I go sometimes to get away from things or just relax when I don't want to be found." When she saw the wry smirk on Clint's face, she blushed slightly and added, "All right. I may not always be alone when I come up here, but I swear to you that I don't drag just anyone here with me."

"Does Jasper know about this?"

"He knows, but he's never seen it. Please," she said with a sudden twinge. "Give me some credit."

"How much money did you make off of this saloon?"

"More than Jasper knows about. And before you lecture me on business ethics, I'll have you know he tried to screw me out of my earnings every way to Sunday, but I caught him each time. Now he's like a little pup that does what he's told and growls when my back's turned."

"And is that why you had to hide me up here when that little pup came scratching at your door?"

Rolling her eyes slightly, she slipped her hands up under Clint's shirt and raked her nails invitingly over his skin. "Sorry about that. I do still need to keep some degree of propriety around here. After all, I am still the boss. It just wouldn't do to have Jasper know what I've got under this dress of mine."

"Still bashful every now and then? I like that."

"I'll bet." She'd already gotten his shirt off and was leaning back while Clint worked on peeling the dress off of her body. "Besides, he just needed to collect the month's earnings to deposit them in the bank. That as well as some other papers that are better off in a real vault rather than that safe of mine in my office. I don't think he knows, but the lock doesn't even work anymore. It rusted out a month ago."

Once the dress came up over her head, Maribeth was naked in front of him. Clint walked her toward the bed and eased her down onto the comfortable mattress. "And you trust him with all that money?" he asked while letting his lips trace a line between her generous breasts.

"Not really, but I have a couple men who work security follow him when he makes these runs whether he wants them to or not. They haven't had to step in on him yet."

"Sounds like you've got this all worked out."

"Of course I do."

"You really have changed a lot since the last time I saw you," Clint said as he crawled on top of her and settled between her open legs. "Now let's see if you've managed to solve this one problem you used to have."

"Problem? What problem?"

"The problem of you screaming a little too loud when I did this."

Clint thrust his hips forward and a little to the side, sliding inside of her while also brushing against a spot that made Maribeth's back arch and her hands grab hold of him with all her strength. The moan of pleasure poured out of her a fraction of a second later.

TEN

When Jasper came out of the door marked PRIVATE, his arms were full and his face was split by a wide, sloppy grin. Every one of his teeth were on display and if more people were watching him instead of the stage show, they might have started laughing at the blatantly comical sight.

One person who wasn't laughing was a thin figure who was leaning against the bar. He held a bottle of whiskey in one hand and his other was resting on the buckle of his belt. The man's eyes were fixed on that door in the back of the room, and when he saw Jasper come waddling through it, he lifted the bottle to his lips and tilted it back.

By the time the fat man was close enough to be heard when he spoke, the man at the bar had set his bottle down and swallowed the mouthful of liquor. Jasper didn't slow down for more than a second. That was all the time he needed to nod toward the front door and point himself in that same direction.

After tossing some money down onto the bar, the other man snatched up his bottle and fell into step behind Jasper. They moved along the edge of two crowds. One group of locals were seated at card tables engrossed in their games while the other, larger group was entranced by the singers and dancers kicking their skirts up onstage.

A few of the patrons acknowledged Jasper with a polite nod or a halfhearted wave, but they were looking back to their own business before the second man could pass them by. Since neither one of the pair was looking to attract much attention, that suited them just fine. They walked through the front door and onto the boardwalk with Jasper still in the lead.

"Hang back as far as you can," Jasper said in a voice that was already starting to wheeze with the effort of his movement.

The second man didn't need to hear another word before doing what he was told. Casually finding a good spot against the outside of the saloon, he leaned against the wall and took another drink as though that's what he'd been planning to do the whole time. He stood with his head tilted down and his shoulders slumped forward, resembling any one of the dregs that hang about outside a saloon.

A dreg that was dressed slightly better than average, but a dreg all the same.

Beneath the brim of his hat, the thin man's eyes remained attached to Jasper like mud on a pig. He didn't plan on letting the fat man out of his sight, which meant he'd have to start walking again once Jasper turned the next corner. Just as he was about to step away from the wall, he was nearly knocked over by a pair of burly young men who'd come bursting out of the saloon in a rush.

After watching for a couple seconds, it became obvious that those two were trailing after Jasper and didn't care who knew it. It was probably safe to say that they didn't think anyone else was watching the fat man, so they had no reason to worry about stealth.

The man with the bottle was used to being overlooked in such a way. In fact, he'd come to expect it when out on one of his jobs. Not that he held it against them. After all, who was going to notice another scrawny figure when they had so many more important things to do?

And even if they did get a look at his face, Ellis Darrow looked much too wasted away and sickly to pose any real threat. If anything, the looks that came his way were filled with more pity than suspicion. After that, the next step was for the person looking at him to quickly turn away and find something else to do that took them in another direction.

This wasn't quite the case this time, since Darrow highly doubted that those two youths even realized that he'd been there. All the better. With that in mind, he lifted the bottle to his lips and took another swig of the fiery liquid inside. He started walking at a leisurely pace behind the two young men, watching their anxious pursuit with no small amount of amusement.

Once Darrow turned the corner himself, he got a clear look at all the players down an otherwise deserted stretch of street. Seeing himself, those two young men, and Jasper all lined up like a stretched-out freight train brought a smile to Darrow's face. The most humorous part of it all was that everyone in that train thought they were being so damned sneaky when the fact of the matter was quite the opposite.

The more Darrow thought about it, the more he considered the option that he might have even had someone following him as well. All he needed to do was take a look behind him and check it out. With there not being anyone else on the street, it would have been simple enough to spot someone trying to follow in his tracks.

But Darrow didn't turn around to look, no matter how simple of a task that might have been.

If there wasn't anyone there, then turning around to look would have been a waste of time and effort. After all, watching Jasper and those two behind him was what he was getting paid to do. And if there was someone behind him, Darrow really didn't want to know about it.

The law would have stormed in already with guns and mouths blazing. Anyone else wasn't any of his concern.

Even if someone else was after Jasper for some reason, Darrow still didn't want to know about it ahead of time. The thought of walking along with his nose pointed forward seemed so much more attractive. Any other players would reveal themselves soon enough.

The only one he needed to concern himself with was the one he'd spotted earlier in the day. It had taken a while for it all to sort through his mind, but Darrow had been able to put a name to the man he'd glimpsed sitting with his feet propped up on the porch of that little restaurant. Having him in town was an interesting twist and to a man that was able to feel every second drain the life from him, interesting twists were the only spices left in life.

Darrow figured he'd take his chances on being followed. He would wager that nobody would think to follow him except for the young guns hired to keep an eye on the fat man. He could just as easily take a more cautious route or even pick off those two specks before they got one step closer to Jasper.

He could, but what fun would that be?

ELEVEN

Jasper clutched his packages to his chest with all his strength. He treated the bundle of papers and the burlap sack the way a drowning man treated a piece of driftwood. Every other second, he shot a look over his shoulder, trying not to stare directly at the two men behind him even though there wasn't much else on the street for him to see.

His breath started to become labored and the sweat began to push its way out through his brow. The bank was directly ahead of him, its doors unlocked despite the sign in the window which read CLOSED. Jasper stumbled up the two steps that took him from the street onto the boardwalk and reached out for the handle on the door. It came open, allowing him to charge inside.

"Evenin', Jasper," said one of the four workers who were wrapping up their daily business. "Want me to help you with those things? You look like you're about to keel over."

Jasper took another couple of steps into the bank and looked around. Although there were only four people scattered around the bank, it felt as if the room was crowded. Jasper didn't feel comfortable with so many workers

around, even if two of them were women and the remaining pair were the scrawny, bookish types one would
expect to find working late inside a bank.

"No, no," Jasper said as he set his things onto a counter
in front of one of the caged teller's windows. "I've got it
just fine." The sweat was still rolling down his face. In
fact, now that he was inside the bank, it was rolling down
his face in a cold, salty stream.

Just then, the doors burst open again and the two young
men from the saloon stepped inside. Both of them worked
security for The Tweed House and they were each built
like oxen. Their eyes were bright and confident, filled with
youthful vigor that only intensified when they compared
themselves to the paltry specimens inside the bank.

"We're closed," said the skinny man who'd been talking to Jasper. His mouth was all but covered by a thick,
gray mustache that looked as though it pulled his entire
face down toward his pointy chin. Stepping out from behind the counter, he straightened the lapels of his brown
suit jacket and walked up to the two new arrivals.

Jasper's eyes went straight toward the back of the room.
Through a half-open door, he could see the vault had been
left open. Another woman stood in front of the large steel
monstrosity and shut the door between the rooms. That
woman brought the total number of workers inside the
place to five.

Damn, Jasper thought. *This is getting to be too much.*

"We're closed," the old bank worker repeated. "Perhaps
you two could come back tomorrow."

The larger of the two young men was named Jeff. He
had stubbly blond hair and a clean-shaven face. His arms
resembled tree trunks and his torso was thick and nearly
round. He smiled in a surprisingly disarming way, displaying a set of straight white teeth. "Miss Tweed sent
us," Jeff said. "We're just s'posed to look after Jasper here
while he makes his deposit."

The old man considered that for a moment and then nodded. "Fair enough. With so much money headed for the vault, I can't say as that's such a bad idea." Turning to Jasper, he said, "Let's have it, then. I hate to rush ya, but my missus is cookin' meat loaf tonight and I'd hate to miss that."

Jasper could feel his guts twisting into a knot. He didn't want those two standing there for this. That wasn't part of the plan. But if he didn't speak up soon, he might just miss his opportunity to follow through on the entire—

"Jasper?" the old man asked, interrupting the fat man's chain of thought. "You all right?"

"Yeah. I'm all right. I just need to . . . that is . . . I almost forgot that I need to make a withdrawal as well."

"A withdrawal?"

Although it was the older man who asked the question, those words were on the lips of the two younger ones as well. Both of the men from the saloon eyed Jasper suspiciously, waiting to hear what would come out of his mouth next.

Taking a deep breath, Jasper calmed himself enough to keep talking without tripping over his words. "That's right. Maribeth wanted me to fetch the proceeds from the last two deposits and count them . . . just to make sure our records are straight." Looking over to the younger pair by the door, he added, "I guess she doesn't trust my arithmetic skills."

Jeff's face twisted with a bit of confusion, and he looked over to the one standing next to him. That one, named Scott, was stouter and slightly rounder than the first. His face displayed a bit more meanness than his partner's and his knuckles were scarred from countless fistfights. His scalp was bald, which made his face look more angular and leaner.

"Miss Tweed didn't say nothin' about no withdrawal," Scott said.

Jasper forced out a sputtering laugh. "Well I'm her partner, boy. And you're hired help. You think she's gonna tell the bartenders and everyone else about the comings and goings of our money?"

Keeping his eyes focused on the two while struggling to keep his face from showing the nervousness that was bubbling up to the surface, Jasper hoped he could back the two down. All the while, his mind raced with one question: Where the hell was Darrow?

By the look on Jeff's face, he couldn't care less about what Jasper wanted to do. Apparently, Maribeth's orders didn't go so far as to explain every last detail. But Scott didn't seem quite so complacent. He scowled at the fat man with open suspicion, clenching his jaw while pondering over what he should do.

"Stay put," Scott said finally. "I'm gonna check with Miss Tweed. And you," he said to the old banker, "don't take nothin' out of that vault."

TWELVE

For a moment, the banker paused. Then, shrugging, he walked back behind the counter. "Be quick about it. I'll finish up what needs to be done, but I won't stay for more'n another half hour. After that, the meat loaf'll get cold."

Scott was about to threaten the old man into staying for however long was required, but he knew that he'd get to The Tweed House and back with plenty of time to spare. Besides, he didn't exactly take kindly to pushing around regular folks who weren't already drunk and throwing punches.

"Stay here," Scott told his partner. "I'll be right back."

Acknowledging the order with a casual nod, Jeff crossed his arms and squared his shoulders so that he was standing directly between Jasper and the front door. The kid could instantly recognize the fear in Jasper's eyes and he would have been lying if he tried to act for one moment that he didn't enjoy it.

The rest of the workers inside the bank appeared uncomfortable by the sudden change in the mood, but they all looked to the oldest man to see how they should react. Since the old-timer in the brown suit didn't seem overly concerned with the situation, they allowed themselves to calm down a bit as well.

After all, it was common knowledge to anyone who spoke with both owners of The Tweed House that Maribeth and Jasper couldn't stand each other. They squabbled constantly and the fat man had nothing but foul words to say whenever Maribeth was out of earshot.

The women gathered together and found things to do away from Jasper and his burly guard. The second male banker, who was only slightly younger than the first and dressed in a plain white shirt and black trousers, whispered some things to those women, which seemed to ease their worries.

With everything seemingly well in hand, Scott turned his back on the fat man and headed for the front door. He stopped short as soon as he'd stepped outside. What caused him to halt so suddenly was the sight of a single figure perched at the edge of the boardwalk. Not only had he not seen the man until that very moment, but he hadn't even heard him walk up the steps.

"Bank's closed," Scott said in a gruff voice. "Come back tomor—"

Before he could finish his sentence, the man in front of Scott stepped forward and jabbed something into the young man's gut. Scott tried to speak, but the only sound that would come out was a labored grunt.

All the while, the man who'd been waiting for him stared into Scott's eyes, twisting his head to hold his gaze as the burly young man started to crumple. He stood fast when Scott reached out to grab hold of him, shrugging off the kid's meaty fists as though he was wriggling out of an uncomfortable coat.

When the man twisted his body and gritted his teeth, Scott let out a louder moan and his entire body convulsed one last time.

All of the eyes inside the bank were looking toward

the door now. All they could see was Scott's back and the slightest hint of the top of the other man's head. But in a matter of seconds, Scott folded over and dropped to the boardwalk. The impact of his body sounded wet, as though the wood beneath him was covered with rainwater.

With the younger man out of the way, the other was revealed. Darrow stood with his arms hanging at his sides. His right fist was clenched around a slender blade that was slick with freshly spilled blood. Shreds of clothing and other remnants of Scott's innards hung from the dagger's edge, connecting the weapon to the wide-open wound of the man dying at his feet.

Already, Scott's body had stopped moving. The planks beneath him were soaked through with blood and his arms were reaching out for the thin, darkly dressed figure.

Darrow stepped over the body as though he was simply avoiding a pile of garbage he'd found on the street. Cleaning the blade with a couple swipes against his pants leg, he tossed the weapon through the air in front of him and caught it with his left hand.

Nobody inside the bank seemed willing or able to make a move until Darrow had stepped inside. Even Jasper, who'd been counting down the seconds for that moment to arrive, looked unprepared for what was going on right in front of him.

"You had business to do, Jasper," Darrow said in a quiet, almost disinterested voice. "Go ahead and do it."

THIRTEEN

The first among the others inside the bank to move was Jeff. Having just managed to shake off the shock of seeing his friend and partner gutted like an animal, he felt every emotion inside of him turn to rage. That rage fueled him on as he clenched his fists and swung himself around to face Darrow.

Darrow looked at the hulking youth, who was easily two or three times his own size. Some might have said that one of the boy's arms was nearly as wide as Darrow's body. The skinny killer didn't take another step toward the kid, but he didn't back off either. Instead, he lifted the knife he was holding, held it out for all to see, and then dropped it back into the sheath strapped to his leg.

"You got something to say, big boy?" Darrow said with a taunting smile. "Come and say it."

For a second, Jeff recoiled. The fact that his size hadn't caused any sort of reaction in his opponent had clearly thrown him off. All he needed to do was think about what he'd just seen and he was surging forward yet again.

Jasper started to shout for Darrow to move. As far as he could tell, it didn't look like his hired killer was going to do anything to get away from the human rhino charging

52

toward the front door. Reflexively, the fat man pressed himself back against the counter, once again clutching his packages to his chest.

As Jeff came closer, Darrow had to crane his neck to maintain eye contact with the kid who towered over him. He saw Jeff's fists cocking back like a massive hammer on the back swing. He saw the gun hanging from Jeff's belt. He even saw the muscles in the kid's arm tense as he threw a punch aimed squarely at his face.

The punch came and rather than step aside, Darrow flicked his eyes toward Jeff's and smiled.

When Jeff's punch landed, the sound of its impact was a muted *thump* mixed with the wet snap of snapping cartilage. Darrow went down like a lead weight and he hit the floor flat on his back.

Everyone inside the bank gasped at the brutal sight.

Even Jeff paused for a second while looking down at the prone figure lying on the ground. Blood dripped from his knuckles, and his nostrils flared with the heat of the moment. He started to surge forward again as though he'd seen Darrow move, but stopped when he saw the devastation of Darrow's face.

"Who is that guy?" Jeff asked as he looked down at the man he'd just laid out.

Darrow's jaw was askew and his nose was pumping blood down his face and onto the floor. His eyes were closed, but his chest still moved with the steady pattern of his breathing. Every so often, a bubble formed in the corner of his mouth before running down to join the rest of the blood in a growing pool.

The rest of the bankers were starting to stir as well. Mostly, they whispered hurried questions to one another while trying to keep themselves from screaming or showing the panic that surged through them. Jasper cleared his throat and turned to look at the old man in the brown suit.

"I still need you to get those things from the vault," the

fat man said. "You know I'm part owner of The Tweed House. Those are my profits too, so go get them."

The old man looked as though he couldn't believe what he was hearing. In fact, he suddenly seemed more stunned by what Jasper was saying than what he'd just seen happen in front of him. "Jasper, a man's dead here. We need to get—"

"You need to get my money! Get it now!"

Recoiling from the explosion of Jasper's voice, the old man looked back to the group of women huddled next to the door leading to the vault room. "Don't go in there," he commanded. "I don't know what's going on here, but something's not right."

"What . . . whatever gave you that idea?"

That last question was spoken in a faltering voice that somehow got stronger with each word. Once again, everyone looked toward the front door and watched in stunned silence as Darrow climbed back up to his feet. Jeff seemed more shocked than anyone else, and he let the thin man stand up before he moved to stop him.

Just as he'd done the first time, Darrow didn't move to get out of the younger man's way. Instead, he locked eyes with Jeff and showed him a wide, bloody smile. "You've got a hell of a punch there, kid." Darrow paused to spit a wad of bloody saliva to the floor. "I'll bet you usually win these fights, don't you?"

Jeff pulled his hand back and took another swing at Darrow. He was going more for speed than power this time, however, but his fist still rocked Darrow back a step or two.

Moving one leg back to keep himself from falling, Darrow took the punch and then let his whole body sag forward. He resembled a weed drooping under the weight of a thunderstorm, but he still didn't fall. When he looked up again, his eyes were clouded and his smile was crooked. There was something else on his face. It was something that looked vaguely like excitement.

"Know what . . . they say about . . . pain?" Darrow asked. "It makes you . . . feel alive. Makes everything . . . sharper. Clearer. Like a drug . . . only more natural."

Jeff pulled his hand back even farther than he had the first time. The look in his eyes was that of murderous rage and with this next punch he clearly intended to remove Darrow's head from his shoulders. "You crazy son of a bitch. I'll show you more pain than you ever thought there was."

Waiting until the last fraction of a second before Jeff's fist plowed through the air, Darrow snatched a pistol from his side and brought it up. The motion seemed freakishly quick coming from someone as damaged and bloody as he. But the gun was drawn and its barrel was pressed against Jeff's forehead before the younger man had a chance to do a damn thing about it.

Darrow let just enough time pass for Jeff to know what had happened. As soon as that realization hit him, the trigger was pulled and the back of the kid's head exploded like a melon that had rolled beneath a wagon wheel.

The air was suddenly filled with a red mist as the bankers let out a collective shout, which was all but wiped away by the thunder of that single gunshot. Jeff remained standing until Darrow pressed the tip of his gun's barrel against his face and pushed him over. The impact of the kid's body hitting the floor could be felt by everyone in the bank.

"You think he feels pain anymore?" Darrow asked. "No. You know why that is? Because he isn't living. I'd say that proves my point."

Jasper appeared to be every bit as horrified by what he'd seen as the rest of the folks huddled inside the bank. His flabby features quivered and his lips shook as though he was struggling to hold back a rush of tears.

"Go on Mr. Prescott," Darrow said as he took hold of

Scott's body and pulled him inside. He dumped the corpse next to Jeff's and then pushed the bank's door shut. "You came here for a reason, let's get to it."

"Oh, y-yes. I came here for a reason." Turning to the old man in the brown suit, Jasper said, "Get to the vault. Get that money and bring out the safe-deposit box that belongs to The Tweed House."

The old man started to protest, but he looked at the bloody visage that was Ellis Darrow. "All right," he said weakly. "I'll do what you say, just don't hurt us."

Jasper straightened his posture and swiped at his forehead. "That's better. This'll all be over soon enough." It was impossible to say if his halfhearted reassurances were intended for the bankers or his own benefit.

FOURTEEN

Clint lay next to Maribeth in the near-darkness of her private bedroom over The Tweed House. They were on the bed, but positioned at a diagonal to where they would normally have been if they were there for nothing but sleep. The sheets were entwined around their arms, legs, and bodies in a mess of soft cotton.

Although he hadn't fallen asleep, Clint felt the kind of groggy light-headedness that usually only comes after waking up or from drinking too much. His body was tired, but in the best possible way. When he started to get up, he heard the reluctant groans of the woman next to him who tried to hold him down with a single hand.

"I don't want you to leave," Maribeth said. "Not yet."

Clint sat up and felt her hand drop down to his lap. That's when he got a look at where they were and the mess they'd made during the last hour.

The comforter was in a ball on the floor and the pillows were still arranged in the strategic piles that were intended to make it easier for them to hold the positions they'd created earlier. The air held the musky scent of sex and it made Clint's mind stray back to the pleasures that Maribeth had given him.

To some degree, he could still feel the chills running through his body and when he looked back to her, his first instinct was to reach out and run his hand along her naked side. She reacted instantly, writhing beneath the sheets and purring with delight.

Rolling onto her back, Maribeth made no effort to keep the sheets from falling away from her and lifted both hands over her head. "Don't start anything you can't finish, cowboy," she said, relishing the way Clint watched as she displayed herself.

"Then I'd better stop now."

"What?" Maribeth's face dropped and she sat bolt upright. "Are you truly that cruel?"

"No, but I am truly that hungry. Where can I get some food?"

"Didn't you eat before you got here? In fact, I know you did! I specifically fed you before bringing you up here so you wouldn't have to leave for any reason until I was ready for you to go."

"Damn," Clint said with a smirk. "You truly are a devious woman."

"You think I got all this from being polite and hoping others would do what I wanted? I've had to learn to think ahead. Everything turns out better that way."

"Well, I must be getting old then, because I feel like I haven't eaten in a week."

The stern look on Maribeth's face quickly faded. Soon, it was replaced by a coy smile as she brought her knees up to her chest and wrapped her arms around them. "Actually, I could use a bite or two myself. How about you go downstairs and tell them to make us something?"

"I thought you said the only cook you employed was at Jesse's."

"No. That's the *best* cook I employ. The lady downstairs cooks well enough to please a bunch of drunks and gamblers. Her stew isn't half bad and it sticks to your bones. Bring me a bowl of it too. Oh! And some bread. The bread goes really well with the stew."

"Anything else?" Clint asked sarcastically.

"Nope. That'll do it. Just tell them to start you a tab. That way I don't have to go down there and vouch for you."

Clint stared at her with mild annoyance. Although he didn't much like playing the part of a waiter, it was hard to resist a woman as beautiful as Maribeth when she was only wearing a strip of sheet and a smile. "I'll be right back," he said finally.

"And I'll be waiting right here." With that, Maribeth scooted back until she could rest her shoulders against the headboard. She moved her hands out to her sides and slowly lowered her legs until she could cross one over the other. The flickering candlelight played over her full, sumptuous curves, drawing his eyes over her breasts and then down to the soft patch of hair between her legs.

"Hurry," she whispered.

It was a test of Clint's will for him to leave that room at all. As if acting out of pure survival instinct, his stomach churned and gurgled loudly, forcing him to rearrange his list of priorities. Clint gathered up his clothes and threw them on. After stepping into his boots, he took one last look behind him before turning the knob of the door leading to the stairs.

Maribeth's eyes were locked on him and she was tracing the fingers of her right hand between her breasts and down to her stomach.

Clint turned around before she could move them any farther. He knew if he didn't leave right then, he might just starve to death before ever getting the strength to leave again. It was a close fight, but his belly somehow managed to win out.

FIFTEEN

The farther Clint got from The Tweed House's attic, the hungrier he felt. Once he got down the stairs and to the end of that short hallway, he found it easier to focus on something else besides getting his hands on that woman again. Not that he was eager to leave her behind, but every man had to eat sometime no matter how inconvenient the timing might be.

Clint was even more distracted from his baser desires once he opened the door leading back into the saloon's main room. The music wasn't as boisterous as it had been since the dancers were no longer on stage, but the small orchestra was still playing a catchy, entertaining tune. To make up for the lack of applause and singing, the rest of the customers were talking in louder voices so they could be heard over each other.

It was only a few steps to the bar, and when Clint got there, he was immediately greeted by a familiar face.

"What can I get for you?" the barkeep asked.

Clint placed the order and was stopped before he requested to start a tab.

With a knowing smirk, the man behind the bar waved his hand and shook his head. "No need for that. I'm sure

Miss Tweed would only tear up your bill the moment she got back downstairs."

Embarrassment wasn't something that Clint was prone to, but he felt the subtle hints of it when he saw that look on the barkeep's face. "You know who I am, huh?"

"Let's just say I know Miss Tweed. By the way she was looking at you, my guess is she wasn't taking you back there to see her office. Besides, the uh . . . other room is . . ." He let the sentence trail off and instead pointed quickly over his head.

It only took a bit of quick figuring for Clint to realize that the upstairs room must have been right in the vicinity of the bar and shelves behind it. In fact, the bed itself might have been pretty close to directly over where the barkeep was standing. For the second time in as many minutes, Clint felt the subtle burn of embarrassment creep under his skin.

"I hope we didn't create too much ruckus," Clint said, even though he knew he and Maribeth had created plenty of ruckus.

"Nah. Did you get a chance to see her office, though?"

Although glad for the change of subject, Clint was still stricken by how suddenly it had come. "No. Actually I didn't get a chance. I will later, though, I'm sure."

"The only reason I ask is because I was wondering if you might know where Jasper got to."

"Maribeth's partner?" Clint asked as he recalled the fat man's face. "I don't know where he is. Why?"

"I saw him go through the door back there and then come out with his hands full."

"Is that unusual?"

The barkeep thought for a moment and then shrugged. "Not particularly, I guess. It's about time for him to make the deposit. But there was something that did strike me as kind of . . . well . . . odd." Suddenly, the barkeep leaned forward and set his elbows upon the bar. He lowered his voice as well, until he could just barely be heard over the general noise of the saloon. "You *are* Clint Adams, aren't you?"

"Yes," Clint replied, not liking the tone in the barkeep's voice. The other man didn't seem to be hiding something, but he did seem to be headed in a direction that wasn't too good. "I am."

"It's probably nothing, but Jasper met up with someone right before leaving here. It was some fella that I never seen before. Jasper said a few words to him and then left so fast I thought his tail feathers were on fire."

"What did this other man look like?"

"Kind of tall. I really didn't get too good a look at him." The barkeep's face brightened for a second and he tapped the bar. "Something I did notice was that he didn't look too good."

"Huh?"

"He was skinny, but a little too skinny. Kind of pale too, like he might've been sick or something."

Clint looked over to the spot the barkeep was talking about as though he thought he might see phantom images of Jasper and his sickly companion standing in their places. "Is it strange for Jasper to meet anyone when he makes his deposits?"

"Actually, yeah. Once he gets his hands on that money, he usually shuffles over to the bank without saying boo to anyone."

"Isn't it a bit late to go to the bank?"

"Not for Jasper. He doesn't like going over there with the deposit when everyone else is there. With Miss Tweed being one of their best customers, I guess the bank doesn't mind giving them a few extra accommodations."

SIXTEEN

Clint looked back to the barkeep and studied the man. He couldn't have been a day over thirty and he had a slender build that made his baggy clothes look like they were still hanging on a rack. "How do you know so much about all of this?" Clint asked.

The barkeep laughed. "Jasper and Miss Tweed fight about damn near everything, but he seemed happy enough when she offered to have a word with the bank manager to keep the place open for him. They talked about it right here before heading to the office. I remember because it was one of the only things I can remember them not fighting about."

"Ok. That sounds like it could be a little strange, I'll give you that. My next question is what do you want me to do about it?"

The barkeep started to say something, but was interrupted by another worker who walked right up to the bar and dropped a tray down right next to Clint.

"Here's the food you ordered," the young girl said.

Clint could smell the stew and felt his stomach gurgle in response. He was hungrier than he'd thought.

Taking the tray and sliding it directly between himself

and Clint, the barkeep started to look uncomfortable. "Those of us that've lived here for a while know what you did for the town a while back and with you here and everything, I thought you'd be able to take care of things a whole lot faster than the sheriff." Mentioning the law, the barkeep straightened up and shook his head. "The sheriff. Fat load of good that one is."

"So let me get this straight," Clint said, trying not to get too distracted by the delicious scents drifting up from the stew. "Jasper went for his normal deposit, but this time he talked to someone else and then hurried out of here."

The barkeep nodded.

"And you didn't like the look of this other person?"

"No, sir," the barkeep said sternly. "Not at all."

"And you want me to . . . track him down for you?"

The barkeep stared back at him as though he was waiting for something else to be said.

Once Clint realized that the other man wasn't following him, he said, "I guess I just don't see what the problem is you want me to look for. It sounds like business as usual except for this other fella and even that could have been a hundred other things."

"It's a gut feeling I guess, Mr. Adams. Something feels . . . wrong. Jasper's been awful quiet lately and he's been drinking more than usual. He seems angry at something and when he starts to talk, he shuts up. That's not like him either." Once again, the barkeep leaned in closer so that he wasn't speaking loud enough to be heard by anyone but Clint. "A man in my job learns to read people. Jasper's eating himself up about something and in my experience, that means he's feeling guilty about something he's done, or something he's about to do. You know what I mean?"

Clint studied the barkeep for a second before nodding. "Yeah. I do know what you mean. Tell you what, as soon as I get this stew in my belly, I'll try to find Jasper and see what he's up to. As far as this other sickly man's concerned, I'll try to find out something about him too."

"That would be great, Mr. Adams," the barkeep said, looking more than a little relieved. "Thank you so much!"

"You think this can wait until I eat?"

"Yeah. Sure, I . . . I guess it can."

Cocking his head slightly, Clint looked the barkeep directly in the eyes and waited.

It didn't take more than a second before the bartender let out a reluctant breath and shook his head. "It's just that Jasper seemed extra worried now and he was in such a hurry after talking to that skinny fella that I really don't think—"

Clint stopped him with a raised hand. "It's all right. I know what you're saying. I'll throw a couple spoonfuls of this down while I'm getting my things from upstairs and I'll be quick about it."

The expression on the bartender's face brought new meaning to the phrase *lighting up*. In fact, he seemed to make a glow that could have been reflected off the polished wooden surface he was resting his hands upon. "Mr. Adams, I don't know how to thank you."

But Clint had already picked up the tray and was headed for the door marked PRIVATE. "You can thank me by being right about this," he said over his shoulder.

Clint ran the food up to Maribeth, pulled on the rest of his clothes and buckled his gun belt around his waist.

Still lying naked on the bed with the sheets strategically positioned over her more inviting parts, Maribeth sat up and watched in shock as Clint rushed about collecting his things. "What's going on?" she asked. "Where do you think you're going?"

"Something's come up," he said. "At least, something had better have come up or I'm going to have a serious discussion with one of your bartenders."

"Which one?" she asked, her voice losing all its softness and taking on the hard-edged tone that reeked of authority. "Was he bald or was he fat?"

Pulling on his jacket, Clint walked over to her and leaned down to kiss her on the lips. "Never you mind about that."

"Don't say that. Not with you picking up and leaving before I get a chance to say a proper good-bye!"

"I'm not leaving. Well, not for good anyway. I just need to run and check on something that might be important. It's about your partner."

"Jasper?!" When she said that, Maribeth jumped up so fast she didn't even realize her sheet had dropped off of her and she was standing completely naked in front of him. Propping her hands on her hips, she asked, "What has he done now?"

"I don't know. Maybe nothing. And if I don't get moving now, I probably won't find out until it's too late. Just trust me on this. I'll come back as soon as I can. In fact, take your time with this meal and give me an hour. If I'm not back by then, wait for me downstairs."

Maribeth walked up to Clint and placed her hands on his shoulders, allowing her arms to drape between them. By now, it was obvious that she was very much aware of her nakedness and was in fact flaunting it as she twitched her hips and moved lively enough to put a sexy bounce in her steps.

"I love it when you boss me around in my own place," she said while nibbling on his bottom lip.

After giving her a quick kiss in return, Clint turned and playfully smacked Maribeth on her bare bottom. "I'll let you know what happens, if anything happens at all."

"And if Jasper is trying to pull something, save him some misery and put a bullet through his fat face for me."

"I love it when you talk rough," Clint said with a wink before leaving the bedroom and shutting the door behind him.

He bolted down the stairs and was passing the bar in no time flat. Stopping in front of the familiar barkeep, he said, "I need to know the quickest way to the bank."

The barkeep gave him hasty directions.

"And tell me your name."

"Marvin," the barkeep said. "Everyone here knows me."

"Good. Because if this turns out to be nothing and you made me leave what I left behind, I'll be coming after you next."

Marvin chuckled as Clint walked away, but only slightly. After hearing the ruckus coming from the attic earlier, the barkeep was sure Clint wasn't kidding about that last part.

SEVENTEEN

The bodies lying on the floor of the bank had all but bled out by the time the old man and Jasper retuned from the vault room. They hadn't been gone for too long, but Darrow had done a good enough job of opening those two young men up that the boards were soaked through in little more than a minute.

All of the remaining bank workers were gathered behind the counter. The women sat huddled on the floor and the younger man stood in front of them where he could offer comforting words in between keeping an eye on the sickly gunman.

For his part, Darrow had kept mostly to himself. He appeared to be perfectly content with leaning against the counter and drumming his fingers as though he was waiting to make a deposit. He also didn't seem to mind the fact that he was standing close enough to two corpses that he could feel the floor getting slick beneath his boots.

Every so often, Darrow would lower his head and cover his mouth with his hand. Soon after that, he'd begin hacking violently until he was nearly doubled over and his shoulders shook with tremendous convulsions.

"Are you all right?" one of the women asked.

Amid the coughs, a laugh could be heard and Darrow lifted his eyes to look at the woman who'd spoken to him. "Do I . . . look all . . . right?" he answered in between coughs.

"Do you have consumption?"

"Never you mind what I have. All you got to know is that I won't be dropping off until after I leave this bank."

That brought the woman's thoughts back to her own situation and caused her to lower her face into her hands so she didn't have to look at any of the atrocities around her. Some of the others reached out to comfort her, whispering about how they were sure Darrow was hurting and that God was punishing him for what he'd done.

Hearing that, Darrow had to smile. He loved listening to religious folks. They reminded him of children talking about the fairies they'd seen in the woods or the monsters under their beds.

So cute.

So naive.

"You come with me, now," Jasper said as he threw open the door to the vault room. When he stepped back into the lobby, he dragged the old man in the brown suit with him.

"You get what you need from him?" Darrow asked after dabbing at his mouth with a handkerchief he'd fished from his pocket.

Jasper nodded. "Yeah. I did."

"And all the money's there?"

"I counted it myself."

"What about the other papers?"

Patting a leather satchel that he hadn't had before, Jasper grinned like a shark that had just sunk its teeth into a fat swimmer. "These are all the papers that declare who the rightful owner of The Tweed House truly is. Without them, it's my word against hers. That is, it would be so long as she's around to give her word."

The fat man truly looked so pleased with himself that he was about to burst his buttons. He spoke to Darrow while ignoring everyone else in the room, including the corpses that were all but floating in their pools of blood.

"Good," Darrow said as he stepped over most of the blood and stood next to Jasper. "Now I've only got three questions. First of all, what's next?"

"Next I have a talk with my partner and give her the opportunity to bow out gracefully. Then I start moving into that big office of hers and take my rightful place as controlling owner of The Tweed House."

Darrow nodded and gave Jasper a genuinely pleased smile. "Sounds good. Now, what do you know about Clint Adams?"

"Clint Adams?"

"And don't try to lie to me, Jasper. You're not very good at it."

"I wasn't trying to lie. I'm just surprised you mentioned him."

"He's here in town isn't he? I've seen him."

"Yes, he's here. He was with Maribeth the last time I saw him, and I don't think you'll need to worry about him for a while. She was about to spread her legs for him like the whore she is when I saw them last."

Smirking, Darrow said, "I hope you're right about that. Adams has a reputation for busting in on things like this."

The fat man snorted and flashed a lewd smile. "They were already getting started when I went to the office to make like I was doing the normal deposit. I know so because I even saw the bitch's underwear lying on the floor outside her office. I told you. She's a crude whore."

Darrow walked over so that he was standing between Jasper and the corner behind the teller windows. "My last question is this: Did you really want to say all of that in front of them?"

Jasper followed Darrow's gaze, which led his eyes to

the scared faces of all six bank employees who were huddled together in a nervous group. The fat man's eyes grew wide and he sucked in a deep breath. He truly looked as though he'd forgotten those workers were there, even though he'd been talking to one of them less than a minute ago.

"Oh my lord," he said, his blubbery face turning the color of a snake's belly. "I didn't mean . . . or . . . I shouldn't have . . ."

"That's right," Darrow said. "You shouldn't have."

The old man in the brown suit held up his hands and shook his head. "No need to worry about us, Mr. Prescott. We won't say a thing."

Jasper looked over to the old man and then to the others behind him. A hopeful look sprang onto his face as he clutched his money and papers for extra support. Before he could open his mouth, he heard Darrow's rasping voice cut through the air like a machete through a spider's web.

"That's also right," Darrow said. "You won't say a damn thing to anyone."

With that, the pale man drew his gun and took aim. One instant, the old man's mouth was dropping open and he was starting to shake his head. The next instant, a shot blasted through the room and the old man's head snapped back like he'd been struck with a piece of lumber.

EIGHTEEN

When he hit the floor, the old man's body seemed twice as heavy as it should have been. It didn't even bounce when it impacted against the boards. Instead, it seemed to stick in place, plastered down by the mushy, crimson paste that had once been the back of his skull.

"I've made enough noise already," Darrow said calmly to the remaining workers in the back of the room. "Don't make any more noise, or you'll be next."

The younger man had his eyes locked on Darrow and couldn't move. One of the women nodded weakly while trying to hold back the tears that burned her eyes. The other woman, however, was too far gone to have even heard what Darrow had said. Her mouth opened out of sheer reflex and her chest swelled as she took a breath to fuel what was surely going to be an ear-splitting scream.

One of those women didn't get a chance to make a sound. Darrow had already stepped up to her and pressed his gun against her temple, pulling the trigger to silence her for good. The other woman was next. By the time she'd hit the ground, Darrow had already drawn his second pistol and was setting his sights on the next worker in line.

• • •

Clint was walking quickly down the street when he got the sudden urge to break into a run. He thought back to what the bartender had said and wished he hadn't taken so much time with Maribeth and getting directions before following up on Marvin's hunch.

He hadn't spent more than a minute or two at the saloon once he'd agreed to check up on Jasper, but even that seemed like too long. He knew only too well about what it felt like to have a bad feeling in his gut concerning a certain situation. He'd had plenty of those before himself, and most of the time there turned out to be a damn good reason behind that instinct.

It didn't help matters much that the instinct in question belonged to a bartender. Next to good lawmen, miners, and bounty hunters, the men in that profession tended to survive on having accurate gut instincts. At that moment, Clint's gut told him to move faster toward the bank and that was exactly what he did.

After turning the corner, he faced an open stretch of empty street, which ended in the unassuming edifice that was the Broken Cross Savings and Loan. The building didn't look like much. Although the closer he got to it, the darker the planks looked on the boardwalk just outside the bank's front door.

Clint covered the distance in hardly any time at all, reaching the steps leading up from the street, where he stopped before charging up to the door. As he'd been running toward the bank, his eyes were focused on the boardwalk outside the door. First he could tell that the wood was definitely darker there, almost as though they'd been stained unevenly.

When he got closer, the darkness looked more like paint had been spilled. As he drew even closer, Clint caught a smell that made his hand drop down to the modified Colt at his side. It was a familiar smell that always reminded him of rust and copper.

It was blood.

He could smell it, and now that he was close enough, he could easily see that it was too thin to be paint and too red and thick to be much of anything else. It was blood alright. And now that he was less than a few paces away from the front door, he could hear a muffled *thump*, which was also only too familiar.

Gunfire.

Clint didn't bother with the steps. Instead, he launched himself up when he reached the boardwalk and landed directly to one side of the door. He kept moving to avoid the window, turning on the ball of his foot until he could press his back against the wall beside the painted glass panes.

Clint didn't waste another second before taking a quick glance through the edge of the window to see what was going on inside that bank. He expected to see men robbing the place and possibly getting ready to make their big break for the outside.

What he actually saw was something far different than that. Although it could very well have been a robbery, Clint's first impression of what was going on was more along the lines of an execution. Maybe even a full-fledged massacre.

Jasper was the first one to catch his eye, simply because he took up the most space. The next man Clint picked out was the one Marvin must have been talking about as the man whom Jasper had been talking to. Pale and wasting away, the man looked as though he shouldn't even be standing. He was doing a lot more than standing, however. In fact, it looked like the skeletal figure was just about to blow an innocent man's head off his shoulders.

Clint's reactions came less than a second after he took his first glance through that window. Acting on instinct,

Clint's hand swung out to one side, smashing the barrel of his Colt through one of the small panes that made up the bank's front window.

Glass shattered and showered onto the floor. Some of it even sliced into Clint's flesh, but he was too busy to feel any of the pain. He took a quick shot into the bank, targeting the skinny man who was raising a gun in his left hand to point at a trembling man that was backed against the far wall. The Colt barked once, causing everyone in the bank to look his way. Although the bullet whipped through the air and dug into the frame of a teller's window, the shot had had the effect Clint was hoping for.

All of the people huddled in the back corner dove for cover. Even the fat man took a few quick waddling steps and dropped to the floor. The only one left on his feet inside the bank was the skinny figure with the sunken face.

Darrow squinted his eyes and peered through the window, catching a glimpse of the edge of Clint's face. "Ahhh," he said as though he'd already forgotten about what he'd been doing before. "It's about time you showed up."

NINETEEN

Since he'd caught the skinny man's attention, Clint kept his Colt trained on him and moved so that he could see more through the window. "Let those people go," he shouted into the bank.

The gun in Darrow's hand was still pointed toward the workers, but only as a kind of afterthought. He let that arm drop without any question and turned around to face the window head-on. Making his way around the counter, he pushed Jasper aside as if he was kicking a cat away from his feet and the fat man scuttled away in a similar fashion.

"Come on in here," Darrow said. "It's starting to smell a bit, but other than that it's not so bad."

"Stop right where you are and drop that gun!" Clint warned. "Let those people behind the counter come out and if you make a move toward them, I'll put you down."

"I'm not stopping them. In fact, I wanted to let them go earlier, but they insisted on doing what I told them not to." Looking toward the workers who were starting to tentatively move around the counter, he added, "Maybe after all of this, they'll learn how to follow orders."

Not one of the bankers could get themselves to look

Darrow in the face. They moved behind him, quickening their pace until they had a straight path to the door. They hardly seemed to notice Jasper as they stepped over and around him on their way to freedom.

Clint moved over to the door and pulled it open. He let Darrow out of his sight for less than a second before moving into the doorway and reacquiring his target. Nodding to the first of the bankers as they approached, he moved aside just enough to let them by. Once they caught the scent of fresh air, they tripled their pace toward the street.

To the man who was the last one out, Clint said, "Find the sheriff and tell him to get over here."

"I will," the man said, swallowing hard and trying not to look down at the blood covering the boards beneath his feet. Finding a reserve of strength, he nodded quickly and said, "I'll fetch him and bring him back as quick as I can."

Not wanting to take his eyes away from the gunman inside the bank any longer than was necessary, Clint studied the killer's sunken, pallid features. "I've seen you before," he said while stepping inside the bank. "Earlier today. Coming out of the doctor's office. You were with a woman."

"That's right. How very observant of you."

"I've got a good eye for such things. Another thing I observed is that you still haven't put that gun down yet. You want to do that, or would you prefer observing me while I put a shot through that pasty body of yours?"

Darrow stopped in his tracks directly over the corpse of the larger of the two saloon bouncers. He put on an expression that an overly dramatic actor might use to display profound sadness. The effect came complete with scrunched eyebrows and drooping lower lip. "Oh, Mr. Adams, making light of my failing health? I'd have thought you were so much better than that."

The more Darrow talked, the stranger the whole situation seemed to get in Clint's eyes. He relaxed his posture and even lowered his gun so that it wasn't pointed directly at the skinny man's face. "Are there any more workers in here?"

Darrow nodded. "Back there," he said, pointing off-handedly with his pistol toward the back of the room. "Behind the counter."

Clint noticed Jasper crawling on the floor, trying to get away from that area like a pig scurrying from a bucket of soapy water. "You! Stay put for a second."

Jasper immediately pressed his face to the floor and covered his head with both hands.

"If there are people hurt back there," Clint said, "help them up and get them out of here!"

"No one's hurt back there!" Jasper screamed into the floorboards. "The ones that're left are dead. They're dead because that crazy bastard killed them! He was going to kill them all if you hadn't showed up! I didn't want this. Not any of this!"

Darrow listened to what the fat man said with a look of mild amusement on his face. In fact, he even rolled his eyes at the last part and let out a heavy, haggard sigh.

Stepping sideways while keeping himself in a duelist's stance with Darrow, Clint turned his body so that his left shoulder pointed toward Darrow while his other shoulder lined up behind the first. That way, if the skinny man did take a shot at him, there was less of a target for him to hit. When he reached the teller's window closest to the wall, he glanced between the bars and quickly spotted the bodies crumpled on the floor, bleeding out through fresh bullet wounds to their heads.

"What the hell is going on here?" Clint asked in a furious snarl. "Somebody better start talking." He wondered what could be taking the sheriff so long to get to the bank, but Clint was even more concerned with what kind of nightmare he'd stumbled into.

Darrow glanced over to Jasper, knowing that it would have been futile to try and get a word in before the fat man started spilling his life story.

Living up to the expectant look on Darrow's face, Jasper began to spew words out of his mouth faster than Clint could understand them. It finally got to the point where Clint had to ignore Jasper's frantic ramblings and focus once again on the gaunt killer.

Clint could hear people running and gathering outside the bank. One quick look through the window, and Clint spotted a vaguely familiar figure wearing a tin star that winked with a bit of reflected light. The killer still hadn't lifted his gun and despite all his moral impulses, Clint wanted nothing more than a good excuse to put that murderous animal out of everyone's misery.

"You want to shoot me, don't you?" Darrow asked.

Clint kept his poker face up like a well-fortified wall. "No. I want to see you locked up like a mad dog and then hung."

"Letter of the law and all that?" Sniffing the air, Darrow smirked and shook his head. "I don't think so. You're a killer. You know better than to trust a system over your own gun. I can smell that on you."

"Can you?" Clint was sure to keep his eyes on Darrow even as the sheriff and a few of his deputies stormed into the bank squawking like a bunch of birds with ruffled feathers.

Darrow nodded. "That's a fact." Letting his gun slip from his fingers, he raised his hands in the air and waited for the lawmen to take hold of him. "And we both know it."

Neither Clint nor Darrow said another word to each other. The bank had suddenly burst to life as the law surged through the door with their guns drawn. In the initial confusion, they came at Clint just as quickly as they came at Darrow, ordering both men to do what they were told or be shot down.

Clint let the deputies take his pistol. He didn't even listen to what the lawmen were saying since he was too occupied by the haunting glare coming from Darrow's sunken eyes. The more he looked at the killer, the less sickly Darrow appeared.

He seemed beyond sick.

In fact, Darrow looked like a corpse that had been dug up and given just enough life for it to walk and talk. When Darrow looked down at the bodies on the floor, he did so without the slightest twitch or hint of remorse.

He looked at them longingly; almost like he was jealous.

TWENTY

Sheriff Anderson was a big man with an expressive face marked by the lines of many hard years. When he offered Clint his apology, it seemed honest enough and he topped it off by holding out a thick hand as a kind of truce.

Only then did Clint realize he was still glaring intensely as the fresh, bloody memories still swirled through his mind. Trying to push those to the side for a moment, he nodded and shook the lawman's hand. "I understand, Sheriff. It was an honest mistake. No harm done."

Slapping Clint's shoulder and letting out a short bark of a laugh, Sheriff Anderson said, "There was almost plenty of harm done. Some of my more eager deputies wanted to shoot through the window before you killed that poor sickly man you had at gunpoint. Luckily, we had some witnesses to point us back in the proper direction."

Clint and the sheriff were standing in the street outside the bank. He glanced around and spotted the middle-aged man who'd escaped from the bank in one piece. When he saw Clint looking at him, the banker nodded solemnly and turned away.

"What happened back there?" Anderson asked. "You mind filling me in?"

"I was just about to ask you the same thing. What took you so long in getting there?"

Anderson's head snapped back as though he'd been rapped on the nose. "I beg your pardon?"

"Don't you or your men patrol this town? Didn't anyone hear shots coming from the bank? Don't you take any measures at all to keep someone from walking in there and opening fire on the place in town that has most of the money in one spot?"

Anderson's face was predisposed to carrying a smile, but the mood behind it changed in a second. Where the grin had been friendly and somewhat apologetic before, it now became edged with a trace of anger. "I know who you are, Mr. Adams, and I remember what you did for this town a while back. But don't think for one moment that I'll tolerate that tone coming from you or anyone else for that matter."

"Well, excuse me if I'm a bit on edge, but I did just stumble upon a slaughterhouse and damn near caught a bullet or two in the process. That tends to put me in a bad mood."

"Fair enough," Anderson said with a subtle nod. "And I'd be right curious to know how you happened to stumble upon this, with it being after business hours and such."

"I got a tip from one of the bartenders at The Tweed House. He told me Jasper was acting strangely after meeting up with someone he'd never seen before."

"And that would be our pale friend?" Anderson asked, while nodding toward the pair of his men that were hauling Darrow down the street toward the jailhouse.

"That's right."

"A bartender? Which one? Was he bald or fat?"

Clint shook his head and felt a grin come onto his face after hearing the same strange question that Maribeth had asked right before he'd left. Suddenly, he remembered that she was still waiting for him to return, and if word had gotten back to her about what had happened, she was probably worried sick. Then again, she could also be on her way to the bank at that very moment to check up on what was going on.

"To be honest with you," Anderson said, "I understand why you'd be upset about all of this. After all, this is the second time you've been under fire in as many visits to Broken Cross. Why don't we go over all of this a little later at my office? Get yourself a drink and come see me whenever it's convenient for you."

Clint nodded. "I'll do that. In the meantime . . ." He held his hand out palm-up and waited.

Anderson reached for his gun belt and removed the pistol that had been stuck in there next to his holster. With a flick of his wrist, the sheriff spun the modified Colt around so he could slap its handle into Clint's waiting hand.

"We've got a lot to talk about, Clint. Try not to take too long in getting to my office."

"I'll be there later tonight, Sheriff. That is, if you weren't planning on going home."

When Anderson looked over at the bank, his smile looked more like an old coat of paint that had seen better days. "After all of this, going home and getting some sleep sounds awful good. Not too likely, but awful good. I'll be there till dawn, I'm sure."

"And I'll check in before then," Clint said. "First off, I've got someone else waiting for an explanation."

TWENTY-ONE

Clint hadn't taken more than one step through the front door of The Tweed House before he had to brace himself or be knocked over. Maribeth came charging at him with her arms out and a panicked look on her face that made him think he was either going to get a strong hug or a massive smack in the face.

Luckily for him, it was the former since he couldn't have properly prepared himself for the latter.

"Oh my god," she said as she wrapped her arms tightly around him and squeezed. "I heard about what happened at the bank. Are you all right?"

"I'm fine, Maribeth. Or at least I will be if you don't squeeze the stuffing out of me first."

She eased up a little bit and smiled. "I'm sorry. Seriously, though, are you all right? I heard there was shooting and that someone even tried to shoot you when you got there."

"Someone's always trying to shoot me. I'm used to it by now."

Taking hold of his hand, Maribeth dragged Clint through the saloon and sat him down at a table somewhere between the gamblers and those who were there to watch

he shows. Although the crowd had thinned a little and
there were some nervous glances thrown his way, business at The Tweed House didn't seem to be suffering.

Maribeth flagged down one of the young women carrying drinks to and from the bar. "You still hungry?" she
asked.

"Now that you mention it, I could use—"

"Be a dear and fetch us a big bowl of stew and some
bread," she said to the server in a way that somehow
seemed more motherly than bossy. "And a beer. You still
prefer beer, right?"

"That's right."

"And a beer." Once the server turned and dashed back
toward the bar, Maribeth reached out and took hold of
both of Clint's hands.

"You look like you could use a drink more than me,"
Clint said.

"Oh it's on its way as well. None of my servers need
to be told that to know what to bring me and when. I
swear they know me like we're all related or something."

Clint let out a deep breath and allowed himself to relax
in the surprisingly comfortable chair. "They all seem to
like you. The workers, I mean. They genuinely like you."

"Is that such a surprise? I mean, look at who else they
have to deal with."

And that brought the conversation right to the point
where Clint had wanted it to go. "Did the bartender talk
to you about what happened?"

"Marvin? Yes. He was the one who got hold of me
when I came down to refresh my drink. He said something
about talking to you and how you rushed right off to
check on what he was saying. I really appreciate you doing that."

"That's not what I meant. I mean, did he talk to you
about Jasper?"

The normally pleasant look on Maribeth's face dark-

ened immediately. Even with all the commotion, there
was a certain lightness about her that never seemed to
fade. Hearing Jasper's name, however, was like a pair of
wet fingers closing around a flame.

"He told me about Jasper," she said. "He told me
plenty. And if I know that son of a bitch, he was going
to clear out everything he could from that vault and make
off with it so he could try and start a place somewhere
else. Like he could actually be successful without my
help."

Clint placed his hand on top of hers and rubbed com-
fortingly as the server came back to the table and dropped
off their drinks. The stew came next and Clint was once
again struck by the inviting aroma that wafted up from
the bowl.

"Are you worried about Jasper?" Clint asked.

"Worried? How?"

"That he was after something besides all the money in
that vault." Clint waited until what he was saying had a
chance to sink in. Thankfully, it didn't take long before
Maribeth pulled her hands back and took hold of her
drink.

"Oh my lord," she said before downing most of her
liquor in one swallow. "You think he might want to . . .
hurt me?"

Before he knew what he was doing, Clint had taken
hold of the wooden spoon and was shoveling the stew
into his mouth. It was hot, but after one bite he had to
keep from devouring the rest instantly. He nodded in between scoops and spoke with a half-full mouth. "That's
what I was asking you."

TWENTY-TWO

Although she seemed troubled by the notion, Maribeth wrapped her mind around it fairly well and didn't seem as though she was going to panic. "We're not on the best terms, but that's no secret. He has a problem with a lot that I do and he talks a lot of harsh words, but as far as hurting someone . . ." She finished her drink. "You met him, Clint. Do you think he has it in him to do something like that?"

"Honestly, no. But that fella he had with him in that bank sure does."

"He hired a killer?"

"You didn't hear?"

Shrugging, Maribeth said, "When something exciting happens, you hear a lot of things. I only listened to half of it before I blocked it out and waited for you to come back and tell me what really happened."

Clint left out some of the harsher details, but gave Maribeth a quick rundown of what happened as far as he could tell. He told her about what he found at the bank as well as his bizarre conversation with Darrow. Not until everything else did he confirm one of Maribeth's worst fears.

"Those two big young guys," Clint said, after giving a rough description of Scott and Jeff. "They worked for you, right?"

Already, Maribeth looked prepared to hear the worst. "Yes."

"It looks to me like they were shot. They're dead."

Her head drooped like a wilting flower and she clenched her lips to fight back the tears. "I never wanted them to get hurt. They always followed Jasper. You know, just to make him know that he couldn't sneak around behind my back when my business was concerned. But I never wanted them to get hurt. They were good boys. I never thought anything like this would happen to them."

"There's no way you could have known."

When she looked up at Clint, she finally let herself relax, and the tears trickled down her cheeks. "I heard they were killed. But then I also heard you might be killed. That's when I stayed put and waited for you to come through that door back to me. When I saw you, I guess I just thought I'd see them come back too.

"Oh Clint. I feel terrible about all of this. If I hadn't sent them off to keep track of that awful man, then they'd still be—"

"Stop right there," Clint interrupted sternly. "You're not responsible for any of this. Do you understand?" When he didn't get an answer right away, Clint reached out and used a finger to lift Maribeth's chin so she could look him right in the eyes. "Understand?"

"Yes. I guess so."

"There's no guesswork about it. Did you have anything to do with what happened at that bank?"

"No."

"Then that means you didn't have anything to do with it. End of story."

She nodded and dabbed at her eyes with the corner of Clint's napkin. Taking that opportunity to continue gorging on the delicious stew, Clint let a comfortable silence fall over the table. It was nice to just sit back and think about nothing but simple things again.

The stew tasted good and the beer was cold.

There were no gunshots and the air didn't stink of blood. All they could hear was the idle chatter of the customers as well as the chiming of glasses clinking together as they were set out on the tables and bar and then collected once again.

Finally, once Clint's spoon had hit the bottom of his bowl, Maribeth took a deep breath and let it out. "So," she said. "What happens now?"

"First of all, I'm going to need another bowl of this stew. This is fantastic." Clint tore off a hunk of bread and started sopping up the beefy juices from the bowl. "Then you're going to think about anything else Jasper might have done that was suspicious. And once I'm done eating, I'm going to the sheriff's so I can have a word with him myself."

Maribeth shifted in her seat before straightening up and steeling herself. "What about Jasper? Is he . . . I mean, was he . . ."

"He's alive. From what I could tell, he hit the ground long before anyone had a chance to shoot him." Even after all that had happened, Clint couldn't help but chuckle at that particular memory. "In fact, I couldn't get him to shut up before the sheriff got there."

They both laughed for a moment and then the server came back with Clint's second helping of stew. He dug into it without waiting and Maribeth watched while sipping from a glass of water.

"Promise me you'll be careful," she said when he was almost done.

"Always."

"I just don't like what I heard about that killer Jasper

hired. Something doesn't seem right about him."

"Yeah," Clint said as the image of the pale man's intense, fiery eyes flashed through his mind. "I know how you feel."

TWENTY-THREE

With the popularity of The Tweed House and after nearly every other enterprising businessman proclaimed their intent to follow in Maribeth's footsteps, the sheriff of Broken Cross did his part to adjust. More saloons meant more drunks just as more card tables meant more gamblers. In turn, more gamblers meant more fights over cheating and more drunks meant more disorderly conduct in the streets.

Sheriff Anderson hadn't had much of an opportunity to bask in the glory of winning the town back at the Gunsmith's side before he had to get used to doing the job on his own. With all those things in mind, he hired more deputies and got an expansion built onto the jail.

The door leading to the new batch of cells was the same size as the one that led to a broom closet. The main difference being that that particular closet could sleep up to two dozen men if pressed for space. Anderson tossed Jasper and Darrow into their own cells at the rear of that new addition. That was mainly due to the fact that Darrow's eyes never stopped drilling through him and his first instinct was to get the skinny murderer as far away from his desk as possible. As for Jasper, Anderson tossed him into the adjoining cell simply because he figured the fat man deserved the worse seat in the house.

Two deputies with rifles setting on their laps sat at the end of the hall, looking in on the prisoners. Neither of the two younger lawmen responded to the cries and pleas that came from the cell. They just kept their eyes open and their head cocked at a disinterested angle, watching with amusement as the prisoner kept pitching his fit.

In fact, although they were enjoying the spectacle, they never showed a single emotion, no matter how much Jasper Prescott squealed and beat his hammy fists upon the new bars.

Ellis Darrow sat on his bunk, slouched over as though he'd passed out. His head and shoulders were wedged against the wall and one foot hung over the side of his cot to rest upon the floor. When he breathed out, the air came from him with a sound that resembled wind rolling through a tomb. His eyes seemed focused on something right in front of his face, but invisible to everyone but him.

"You did this," Jasper said after slamming the side of his foot against the bars one more time. "This is all your fault. If you hadn't gone crazy in that place, we both would have been riding the hell out of this town."

All Darrow did in response to that was shake his head.

"And don't tell me about our plan, because that was never part of our plan," Jasper went on. "I didn't want any of those people murdered if it could be helped at all."

"Is that so?" Darrow said.

"Yes. That is most definitely so."

"And what did you think they were going to do after they heard all those things you said? In fact, what did you think they would do once they saw how friendly you were to me? Was that part of your plan also?"

The fat man started to speak, but he stopped himself. For the first time in hours, he became voluntarily silent.

Darrow laughed at that and got to his feet. The effort of standing up almost seemed too much for him, but after a few labored breaths, he straightened up and walked over to the bars of his cell. "You knew what you were getting in to. You just didn't have the stomach for it." Glancing over at the neighboring cell, he added, "I'd say that's about the only thing you don't have a stomach for."

The insult rolled off Jasper's back like water off a duck. He jabbed a finger toward the killer and forced a snarl onto his face even though it was clear he was about two steps away from breaking into tears. "You were supposed to handle the workers and deal with the law. That's all you were supposed to do."

"You want to shut your mouth or would you rather start from the beginning so our deputies down there can catch the entire story?"

"It's too late to worry about that. They know all there is to know because you didn't hold up your end of the bargain."

Although he didn't move quickly, Darrow turned his head until he could lock both eyes on to Jasper's blubbery face. When he fixed the fat man with his stare, Jasper recoiled in surprise as though he'd been struck across the cheek.

"I was taking care of the crowd just fine," Darrow whispered. "And if you don't quit your talking real soon, I'll take care of you in the same way." He waited for a couple seconds to see if Jasper was going to try and test the waters with a stray word or insult.

Apparently Jasper had some sense of self-preservation because although he tried to maintain his bad look, the only thing that came out of his mouth was a throaty wheeze. His chest rose up and down and sweat poured down his face even though he'd been off his feet for some time.

"This isn't over," Darrow promised. "Nothing is over

until I can't draw another breath." With his eyes still locked on Jasper, Darrow convulsed as though he'd been hit in the stomach. His eyes suddenly turned bloodshot and his lips began to take on a disturbingly bluish hue.

The coughing fit that followed started out as if Darrow was trying to clear his throat. In a matter of seconds, he was hacking so violently that he had to hold on to the bars in front of him just to keep from falling to the floor. His head drooped and his eyes glazed over as the desperate breaths he'd been sucking down suddenly stopped.

"Good lord," Jasper said as he flopped around trying to get to his feet. "What's the matter with you?"

But Darrow couldn't answer. By the faraway look in his eyes, it looked like he might not have even heard the question. And judging by the trembling in his hands and arms, it was a good bet that he was barely able to hold on to the bars strongly enough to keep himself upright.

The deputies were already responding. Both men ran down the hall, leaving overturned stools behind them. They got to Darrow's cell in a few seconds and one of the lawmen bent at the knees so he could try and look into the killer's face. The second deputy was drawing his pistol just to make sure he could cover his partner, but he wasn't quite fast enough to clear leather before Darrow's eyes snapped open and his hand reached out from between the bars.

TWENTY-FOUR

Sheriff Anderson stepped out of his office a few minutes after making sure the two new prisoners were tucked away in their cells and under guard. He kept the door to his office open so he could hear anything that went on inside there and he was close enough to the jailhouse that he could be there in less than half a minute as well.

All of those precautions were reflexive, however, and he barely had to think about them when he went through those motions. In fact, even with all that had happened and all the bodies that had to be cleaned up from the bank, his mind was on another matter altogether.

The blood that had been spilled weighed heavily on his conscience, but there was something else that pressed down on him like a cart full of bricks. If that other matter wasn't handled properly, it might just mean the end of his career as a sheriff, not to mention his standing in the community as a respected citizen.

Even with all that in mind, he couldn't help but feel excited when he saw the familiar figure turn the nearby corner and start walking toward his office. He kept his eye on the slender shape as it drew closer, part of him wanting to go back inside and forget about it while the other part kept him from looking away.

His first instinct was to check the rest of the street to see if anyone else was around. Even on a normal night, the streets would have been fairly clear. But on a night where the shots might as well have been echoing in the alleyways and the gunpowder could almost be smelled on the air, the streets were downright deserted.

Every so often, a face could be seen peeking around a corner or at the edge of a window, but the moment Anderson looked its way, the face ducked back into hiding. He knew what the locals wanted. They wanted to get a peek at the prisoners or maybe even have that skinny, sickly killer shoot a glance in their direction.

Of course it was morbid, but the lawman had been around such things long enough to know that that was a part of human nature. He'd wanted to see his own fair share of blood also. Namely, he wanted to see that murderer's blood flow from his veins after taking a bullet from the sheriff's side arm.

Even as he thought such things, Anderson shook his head and dismissed them straightaway. He'd seen his fair share of human nature, but he'd also seen more than his share of blood. No matter how much they deserved it, a dead man was not a sight that sat easily in another man's soul.

The sheriff was still thinking about all the gruesome sights he'd been forced to live with when that familiar figure made its way over the boardwalk until it was close enough to touch. Before he got a chance to raise a hand, the figure reached out and touched him. Just a light brush of fingers over his face before the familiar voice drifted into his ears.

"What's the matter, Sheriff?" Ann DiGrasse asked. "Did everything go all right with that terrible business at the bank?"

As much as he wanted to answer her question right away, the lawman shrugged away from her touch and stepped back. "Not here," he said in a whisper that barely caused his lips to part. "Come on." With that, he nodded toward the side of the building and started walking.

Ann followed him as he walked past the front door of his office and kept going until he hopped down off the edge of the boardwalk and turned into the alley. More than just the space between two buildings, the alley next to the sheriff's office was wide enough to let a wagon pass through, which was used mainly for prisoner transfers to the nearby jailhouse.

At the moment, the alley was empty except for piles of old crates and garbage containers stacked along both sides. The shadows were especially thick in that alley and swallowed both the sheriff and his raven-haired companion almost immediately.

"What's wrong?" Ann asked with concern in her voice. "You're starting to scare me a little with all of this."

Anderson began pacing the moment he was away from the street. He took his hat off with one hand while using the other to run repeatedly over the top of his head. "You got no reason to be scared," he said. "You didn't do anything wrong."

"Are you sure? Because the way you're acting, I feel like I—"

"Did you tell anyone about what you were doing?"

She appeared to be a little shocked at being interrupted so suddenly, and shook her head. "No. I— what is this about?"

"Did anyone know that we were together when everything was going on at that bank?"

Smiling and lowering her head as though suddenly embarrassed, Ann lowered her voice and looked around much as the sheriff had been doing when he was scanning the street. "Of course not. I didn't even know that was going to happen until we were . . . well . . . you know."

"Yeah. I know." Another wave of memories flashed through his mind no matter how hard he tried to fight them back. Even though they were much more pleasant than the ones that had been there before, these newer memories stung him deeper than the ones soaked in blood.

They chewed at him just as they had been to some degree or other ever since he'd charged around the corner and seen those bankers staring back at him with their wide, terrorized eyes. Anderson could still hear the frantic voice of his deputy calling for him outside the window of the Three Star Hotel. And no matter how much he tried to shake it from his mind, he could still see the blood that had soaked into the dirt outside the bank as well as the trail which led over the dusty boardwalk through the front door.

The smell of death hung in his nostrils and filled the inside of his head. The only thing that seemed to push it out of him was the enticing aroma of Ann's perfumed skin. God help him, he could still take some pleasure from that.

"It's all right," she said, easily picking up on what was going through his mind. "You didn't do anything wrong. You got there as fast as you could. You had no way of knowing what was going to happen."

Sheriff Anderson took a bit of comfort from that. "No, I didn't. Neither of us did."

Resting her head on his shoulder, she grinned in the darkness and said, "That's right. We had no idea."

TWENTY-FIVE

It wasn't even a day ago.

Hell, it wasn't much more than a few hours ago when everything in Sheriff Anderson's life had been just about as good as it could be. He had a good job, a decent family life, and the respect of his friends and neighbors. Not only that, but he had security and he didn't really even have to do much to keep things on the proper track.

Being a sheriff wasn't too hard. Not in Broken Cross anyway. Although Clint Adams had gotten most of the glory for rousting that bunch of scallywags not too long ago, the locals still looked to Anderson as their leader once Adams had picked up and left. It steamed the sheriff's hide that a gunfighter could swoop in and show him up like that, but then again Adams had taken the risks once he stood up against those outlaws that had been making things so difficult.

Before too long, Anderson was right where he wanted to be: in the driver's seat with reins firmly in hand. And that had been the way things stayed all the way up to this very night. Sheriff Anderson was once again the authority of Broken Cross and to make things even sweeter, outlaws were steering clear of the town as though it were infested with the pox.

Earlier that night, Anderson had been putting away the last of his free drinks at one of the smaller saloons in town when he was flagged down by one of his deputies. The kid's name was Eric and he was fresh enough to the job that he was still stuck with taking care of little jobs such as ferrying messages to and from the office.

Still eager to fulfill his duties as best he could, Eric ran past the saloon before coming back and stepping through the door. "There you are," he said breathlessly. "I just about passed you up before I saw you in the window."

The sheriff liked the kid and encouraged him whenever possible. That way, he figured Eric wouldn't mind if he kept drawing the short straw where duties were concerned. "Great, Eric. Now what's got you in such a hurry?"

"Someone was asking for you back at the office and the others told me to find you and let you know."

"Is it someone important?"

"I'm not sure."

"How come none of the others could handle it?"

"Because she seemed pretty determined to talk to you and you alone. I was there and she wouldn't talk to no one else but the sheriff."

"She?"

Eric nodded. "She said she needed to talk to the sheriff and that it was important. Other than that, she wouldn't say much else about anything."

Anderson's interest was piqued. It was common knowledge among the deputies who had been working under him for any real amount of time that the sheriff enjoyed the company of women. Not only that, but he particularly enjoyed the company of women other than his wife who could keep a secret. That fact was important when it came time to find the town's head lawman in case of emergency and he wasn't in any of the saloons.

"What did she look like?" Anderson asked.

Eric opened his mouth to speak, but stopped and turned quickly to look outside. "See for yourself," he said while pointing down the street. "That's her headed this way."

Setting his glass down and stepping outside, Anderson got a good look at Ann DiGrasse as she strutted across the street while hiking up her skirt so as not to get her hem dirty when she moved. Her long hair rustled in the wind and it was black as coal. She had a tight, firm body with curves that were accentuated by her dress, which hugged her figure on top and flowed only slightly looser around her hips and legs.

When she looked up and caught his eye, Anderson thought he could feel her gaze sweeping over him. She must have seen his badge glinting in the light because she smiled and changed course so she could head straight for him.

Leaning against a post outside the saloon, Anderson waited for her to get to him and enjoyed every last second of her trip across the street. She stopped in front of him all too soon, extended her hand and let her dark red lips widen into an even bigger smile.

"I'm Ann DiGrasse," she said in a full, confident voice. "I take it you're Sheriff Anderson?"

"I certainly am," Anderson said while taking hold of her hand and giving it a polite shake. "And to what do I owe this pleasure?"

Her eyes widened somewhat and she stepped up onto the boardwalk. Before she would speak again, she looked over to Eric who had been watching her from Anderson's side and shifted on her feet.

"Go find something to do, Eric," the sheriff said with unmistakable finality. "And tell the boys back at the office they did a good job."

"I'll do that, sir." With that, Eric nodded and jumped down to the street, eager to get on with his next set of menial duties.

Waiting until the deputy was good and gone, Ann said, "He sure is eager, isn't he?"

"We all started out that way. Then you hit my age and you start getting your priorities in order. My first adjustment was running."

"Running?"

"I don't do it anymore. Not if I can help it. Whatever it is I used to run for will still be there if I walk to it."

They both had a little laugh at that one. Ann threaded her fingers through her hair and tilted her head in such a way that even a blind man could tell she was interested. Anderson could tell so much, in fact, that he almost forgot what had brought them together in the first place.

"So why were you looking for me?" he asked.

She looked down a bit, and then raised her eyes so she could watch him in a way that was sexy and coy all at the same time. "I heard about what you did to save this town. Everyone in these parts has heard. I'm in trouble from an old suitor who's threatened me and follows me around. I guess you could say I need a big, strong lawman to protect me."

A blind man might have known she was interested, but even a deaf one would have thought to question that story of hers. Sheriff Anderson was neither of those things, but he was still most definitely a man. When she looked up at him with her smoldering eyes, Anderson could feel her gaze sweeping down his chest. Her eyes lingered a bit longer than what might have been appropriate once she reached the area below his belt.

Her hands reached out for him, brushing over his jacket and slipping beneath the lapels. She lingered a bit there, as well. Appropriate or not, he wasn't about to do a damn thing to stop her. This wasn't the first time Anderson had seen a woman look at him with the same admiration she might give a gunfighter or some other dangerous type. Although he knew the facts better than anyone, he wasn't about to use them to spoil his chances of grabbing some glory of his own.

He'd never let the facts stop him before. Why start now?

"Protection, huh?" he said, stepping closer to her. "I'm not in the bodyguard business, ma'am."

"Then could you do me the favor of escorting me to my room? I know that scoundrel could be here watching me, and if he sees me with a famous lawman like yourself, he'll think twice about doing anything bad to me."

"We couldn't have that, now could we?"

She shook her head slowly, causing her black hair to dance seductively around her face. "Perhaps you could make sure my room at the hotel is safe as well?" Dropping her voice to a whisper, she added, "And, if you have the inclination, you could be the one doing bad things to me."

Anderson tipped his hat and offered her his arm. "All in a day's work."

TWENTY-SIX

If Sheriff Anderson had known that he was less than an hour away from being summoned to a bank filled with blood and corpses, he never would have gone to that woman's room. As far as he'd known, it was just any other day and she was just any other woman attracted to a man who carried a gun and knew how to use it.

Of course, Ann DiGrasse wasn't just any other woman who was excited at the prospect of being touched by hands that had taken a life. She made the sheriff feel more eager to be with her in less time than it had taken any of those other women in his past. But what really separated her from him was the fact that she did know what was going to happen at the bank.

She knew because she was a woman who was excited at the prospect of being caressed by a killer's hands. Only she didn't feel that stirring inside of her when the sheriff began making his clumsy attempts to arouse her. Perhaps she was spoiled by all the attention she was used to getting from Ellis Darrow. Or perhaps she was spoiled because there was so much more blood soaked into Darrow's hands than Sheriff Anderson had ever seen in his life.

But there was no way for the lawman to know such things. In his mind, this was just any other day and she was a beautiful, exotic woman who wanted him to share her bed. That last fact became obvious the moment they'd gotten to her room at the Three Star Hotel. As soon as the door was closed, Ann shrugged out of the wrap that had been hanging over her shoulders and moved slowly toward him.

He was used to having to do more of the work with women like these. Usually, he had to rattle off a line of stories involving his epic battles with bloodthirsty outlaws over a string of several drinks. That was normally enough to lower their defenses. But this time, he was the one being seduced and he would have been lying through his teeth if he said that he didn't enjoy the hell out of it.

The moment she was close enough, Ann placed her hands upon his shoulders and massaged his knotted muscles. All the while, her eyes never left his. She watched as he began to respond to her and when he reached out to touch her, she leaned her head back and let out a long, contented sigh.

"I've been waiting for that since I first saw you," she said. The sleeves of Ann's dress were off her shoulders, exposing smooth, pearly skin. Slowly, she raised her hands until they were resting on top of Anderson's. From there, she guided him down until his palms brushed against the sides of her breasts.

The moment he could feel the soft, yielding flesh beneath her clothing, Anderson leaned all the way in and kissed her fully on the mouth. His hands moved on their own, grabbing hold of her as though he was compelled to feel more and more of her body.

She moaned in his ear, urging him onward as he pulled down the front of her dress until his fingertips brushed against her erect nipples. Before either of them knew what was happening, they moved over to the bed and were falling down onto the mattress.

Ann was back up and on her feet almost immediately, smiling at him and pushing him down roughly when he tried to get up. "You stay right there," she said. "Let me take care of you for a while."

Anderson didn't want to stay put. The only thing he did want was to take her in his arms and run his hands all over her body. He wanted to peel her clothes off and lay her down so he could crawl on top of her until his every need was sated.

But Ann wasn't about to let him do any of those things. She could feel the tension in his body. She could feel him trying to fight against her and get back up no matter how much she held him down. She knew what he wanted and that showed in the wicked smirk she showed him just before lowering herself down to her knees in front of him.

Once she was sitting on the floor with her legs tucked neatly beneath her, Ann peeled the dress all the way off her body and let it fall into a pile around her knees. The material formed something like a pool of soft fabric with her in the middle of it all. Her bare skin was soft and smooth, seeming almost luminescent in contrast to the striking blackness of her hair.

Ann moved her hands up along his legs, stripping him out of his pants and boots. Moving her fingers up along his thighs, she leaned in until he could feel her hot breath on his lower abdomen and then the base of his penis. She kept her hands moving over his body, her fingernails scraping slow, gentle circles over his chest and stomach while she teased the tip of his cock with her lips.

Watching all of this for as long as he could, the sheriff finally let his head fall back onto the mattress. He wanted to feel his fingers running through that thick, silky hair and by the time his hands got down to her, Ann had already taken him into her mouth.

TWENTY-SEVEN

Her lips parted and she lowered her head all the way down, not closing in around him until her lips could circle its base. Once there, she moved her tongue back and forth and up and down, circling him the way she would a stick of candy.

Anderson's mind couldn't hold on to a damn thing by that point. The room seemed to circle around him and the only thing that mattered was that Ann didn't stop what she was doing. Her head bobbed up and down in his lap at a faster pace. Every time she went down, she devoured his cock as though she was hungry for it. Every time she came back up, she sucked him loudly as if she didn't want to let him go.

Somewhere in the back of his senses, Anderson could hear a ruckus outside. It almost sounded like a whole mess of people running back and forth in front of the hotel. There were also some voices raised, but nothing so loud as a scream or cry for help. All of that sparked his interest and made him tear his eyes away from the brunette for the first time since she'd started pleasuring him.

Ann heard the noises as well. Letting him slide out of her mouth, she reached up with one hand and ran her fingers lightly along the side of his cock while following with the tip of her tongue. She used her other hand to reach into the folds of her discarded dress and fish out a small silver locket from one of her pockets.

When she popped open the locket with her thumb, she turned her face to look down at a small watch built into the locket's lid. The entire process took only a matter of seconds and by the time she was licking upwards again, the locket was closed and secreted away.

It was about that time, she knew. Everything was going according to schedule, which meant that she needed to keep the sheriff busy for a little while longer.

"It sounds like there's trouble out there," Anderson said.

Even though he hadn't tried to get up just yet, Ann could feel the sheriff tensing as he kept trying to get a look out the nearby window.

"You should be more worried about the trouble in here," she said. "Because there's going to be a whole lot of it if you move from that spot."

She stood up and ran her hands down along her body. Working her way down from the sides of her breasts, she had Anderson's complete attention by the time both hands were sliding between her legs. Opening her knees slightly, she eased two fingers from her right hand over the contours of her vagina. After parting the slender lips, she then rubbed the pink nub of her clitoris and let out a satisfied groan.

At that point in time, it was plain to see that Anderson couldn't have remembered his own name, not to mention whatever was happening outside. His eyes were glued to Ann as though there were invisible strings connecting them to her wandering fingers.

She eased closer to him while still touching herself, the moisture between her legs starting to glisten in the light. Turning around, she moved her hands to the small of her back and then rubbed all the way down over her tight buttocks. Ann could hear him moving behind her, but she kept him in his place by backing up until she felt his hard shaft grazing her backside.

Bending deeply at the waist, Ann lifted up just enough as she moved so his cock rubbed over her buttocks and then moved along the lips of her pussy. She backed up just a bit more while lifting one foot up onto the edge of the bed. From there, she lowered herself down and moaned loudly when his cock slid inside of her from behind.

From where he was sitting, Anderson got a breathtaking view of Ann's back as she started riding his cock and tossing her hair from side to side. She had both hands pressed against her knees for support as she bounced up and down on top of him. The curve of her spine was accentuated by a single bead of sweat which emerged from her shoulders and rolled all the way down her back.

It seemed as though Ann was unaware of anything else in the room besides the man she was making love to. Her muscles tensed and her nails bit into the sheriff's skin as she concentrated solely on taking his cock inside of her again and again.

Once she'd felt him drive into her body, Ann clenched her eyes shut and actually started to enjoy what she was doing. Not that she'd been hating it before. In fact, the lawman really wasn't too bad in that respect. But as the time had worn on and Ann knew what was going on outside, the passion became that much more intense.

Just knowing what Darrow was up to while she kept the lawman occupied was already enough to start the first embers of her orgasm building within her body. But now that she could hear the people running around outside and sense the urgency that had suddenly gripped the sheriff's body, she felt those embers start to burn. Ripples of pleasure coursed beneath her skin, which made her want to fan the flames that much more.

She clawed into Anderson's legs and pushed her foot against the side of the bed as though she was going to climb off of him. When she felt that he was about to slip out of her, she spread her legs open and dropped herself down, groaning as he slammed inside of her.

Anderson groaned as well, arching his back and savoring the way he was all but helpless beneath Ann's insistent body. She rode him hard and started screaming loudly as the lips of her pussy clenched tightly around the base of his cock. Just then, he swore he heard something else coming from outside. It was faint beneath the sound of Ann's cries, but he swore he heard a familiar voice calling his name.

Part of him knew he had to get up and see what was going on. He'd known that for a few minutes, but the rest of him kept him pinned to that bed like a pair of strong, invisible hands. Anderson started to try to get up, but as soon as he got his upper body raised off the mattress, Ann only used that as a way to take him inside of her from a slightly different angle.

She knew exactly what he was trying to do. In fact, she'd been listening to those voices outside even more closely than he was since she had to know exactly when to cry out louder to cover them up. When she felt Anderson start to get up, she reached up behind her head and drove her fingers through his mussed-up hair.

Leaning back slightly as Anderson sat up, she pressed her shoulders against his chest and ground her hips back and forth with him all the way inside of her. Not only did she stop him from moving another inch, but she was able to rub the shaft of his penis along a spot that literally sent chills throughout her entire body. From that position, Ann immediately started to climax and her screams took on a whole new level of raw passion.

"Oh god," she screamed. "Oh god, stay right there! Don't move!"

Even if he'd wanted to move, Anderson wouldn't have been able to escape her arms and legs without serious injury to himself. He could feel the muscles in her back, thighs and vagina all contracting as one. The sensation wasn't quite enough to wipe away the voice that he could now clearly hear shouting for him, but it was damn close. The only reason he could still hear it at all over the pounding of his heart was that the voice was now coming from directly outside the hotel room's door. Also, it was being accompanied by a furiously pounding fist.

But Ann wasn't about to stop moving. She'd choked off her screams, but that was only because she was in the powerful grip of her orgasm. Her hips thrust back and forth in a quick rhythm, which was more than enough to push Anderson over the edge as well.

It didn't matter how many deputies were calling his name or pounding on his door. It probably wouldn't have mattered if the whole damn hotel had caught on fire. Nothing would have been able to get the sheriff off that bed until Ann decided it was time to do so.

And by the time she decided to let him go, Ann knew it was already too late for the sheriff to save that bank.

TWENTY-EIGHT

Looking back on that time in the hotel room with Ann, Sheriff Anderson couldn't help but feel himself responding to her again now that she was close to him. The darkness in the alley wrapped around them and made it that much easier to concentrate on her and her alone. He could smell her as she stepped in closer and started to move her hands over his chest once again.

"Stop it," he forced himself to say. "That's the kind of thing I wanted to talk about to begin with."

Ann looked a little surprised as she backed away. "Are you angry with me?"

"No. I'm angry with myself. I shouldn't have been in that room with you. And because I was there, I might have been responsible for all those people getting killed today. My deputies were trying to get me, but instead of doing my job, I was—"

She stopped him by kissing him suddenly on the lips. When she spoke to him, all of the coyness was gone from her voice. She spoke with confidence and strength, assuring him by her tone that not only did she know exactly what was happening, but that she was in control of it. "You were in that room with me and there's no way to

112

take it back now. If you're worried about me saying anything to make you look bad, don't let that get to you. Just worry about doing your own job and everything should work out fine."

Although that had been pretty much what Anderson was going to say, he found he wasn't too relieved to hear Ann say it instead. "So where are you going now?" he asked, mainly because he couldn't think of anything else to say.

"I'm going along my way. Other than that, does it really matter?"

"No. I suppose it doesn't."

"Good." With that, she kissed him once again and stepped away. The smile on her lips was unmistakable, even in the thick, soupy shadows that seemed to grow darker by the second. "I thought I might have seen some busybodies watching me as I walked in here, so I'll leave now and give them something to see. Come on out after a minute or so. That should give me plenty of time to clear things up for you."

Anderson couldn't decide whether he should be grateful or disturbed that Ann was so good at sneaking around and such. Since he figured this was the last time he'd see her, he decided to let her do this one last thing and wash his hands of her completely. "All right," he said. "Thanks."

"No, Sheriff. Thank you."

Watching her turn sharply on her heel and flip her dark mane over her shoulders, Anderson licked his upper lip with the tip of his tongue. He could still taste the salty sweetness of her kiss, which brought back a whole flood of memories from what felt like so long ago.

He knew he should have felt more guilty for what he'd done. Actually, the more he thought about what he should have been doing instead of being in that hotel room, the more his conscience pressed down upon him. The odd part was that all he needed to do was focus on the glorious sight of Ann's naked body writhing on top of his own and he felt instantly better.

Perhaps that wasn't so strange. After all, enough fine wine could make the worst meal go down a hell of a lot better. What had happened at the bank earlier had left an awfully bad taste in his mouth. But then again, Ann was one hell of a fine vintage.

After everything was said and done, Sheriff Anderson still figured he'd managed to come out ahead in the deal.

Ann emerged from the alley, her stride quickly evolving into a strut. She could feel her hips shifting like a cat's beneath her skirt and didn't have to look back to know that the hapless lawman had been watching her the entire time.

She turned the corner and took a quick look at the street around her. Just as when she and the sheriff had ducked into the alley, there weren't any eyes watching her that didn't pull away as soon as they thought they'd been spotted. But she didn't give a damn about any of that. The only thing that mattered was that she had a schedule to keep.

Once again, her hand darted into the little pocket in her skirt. She removed the locket timepiece, flicked it open and glanced down at the miniature hands. She wasn't interested so much in the time of day as she was in how much time had elapsed since Darrow had been tossed into jail.

They'd gone through these motions several times in the past. Ellis Darrow might not have been the most careful of men, but to answer that, they'd worked out a system that served them well enough. If certain things happened while they were on a job, Ann was supposed to take care of certain things to give him time to fix it. Once that time was up, she was to either disappear for a while, or arrange to meet him nearby.

The time to meet him was quickly approaching and Ann could feel it throughout her entire body. She felt a flutter in her lower body that had been there since she was keeping the sheriff out of Darrow's way. The entire time that lawdog had been inside of her, she'd been imagining it was Darrow's cock that she was riding.

In her mind, she was focusing on the fact that Darrow knew what she was doing. When she'd imagined him watching her and the sheriff, her orgasm had become that much more intense. Even thinking about it as she walked down the street was enough to make her have to stop for a second while the little ripples of pleasure worked their way through her system.

Ann didn't stop and dally for long. There was still a job that needed doing and she could hear the sheriff starting to stir in the alley behind her. Thinking that the lawman would be content where he was for a little while yet, she strolled casually inside the sheriff's office and took a look around.

Immediately, she spotted what she needed to find. It wasn't going to be easy, but fortunately there was already a distraction in progress.

TWENTY-NINE

When the deputy had been approaching Darrow's cell, he felt certain that he and the other young lawman were the ones in charge. They rushed over to the sickly man, their youthful vigor charging their feet like steam driving a piston. The distance was covered almost instantly, and they were even careful enough to slow down a bit before getting too close to either of the prisoners.

They worked it just the way Sheriff Anderson had taught them. One man moved up to the bars while the other stayed behind to cover him. The second deputy's hand was even on the grip of his pistol just in case something out of the ordinary happened. Of course, neither one of the deputies were expecting anything to happen since the man they were checking on looked like he was knocking on death's door anyway.

As far as feeling like he was in control of the situation, all of that ended the moment Darrow's eyes snapped open. The prisoner still looked as though he had one foot in the grave, but the burning intensity in his eyes said that he wasn't going into the abyss all by himself.

Darrow's lips parted in a cruel smile and once he had a firm grip on the front of the deputy's shirt, he hacked up a wet cough which sent a sticky load of blood up into his mouth. The lawman was struggling in the killer's grip, already reaching for his gun. But by the time he dropped his hand down to the pistol's handle, he felt the top of Darrow's hand instead.

This time, it was the deputy's turn to stare with wide eyes. Even though each second seemed to drag by, he knew that hardly any time at all had passed. He could only hope that his partner was getting ready to shoot that crazy bastard from behind him. He started to shout for the other deputy to hurry up, but his body was working on normal time, which meant that he was nowhere near fast enough to do much good.

Reaching through from between the bars with his other hand, Darrow plucked the gun from the deputy's holster and snapped the hammer back. The young lawman was starting to say something and twist away, but Darrow hung on with twice as much strength than he should have had.

As always, he would feel this exertion of his muscles in the morning. Hell, even when he tried standing up and sitting down too many times in a day, he was aching the next morning. But that was what life was all about. Well, his life, anyway.

Rather than think too long about what he was doing and how smart it might have been, Darrow turned himself over to the one thing that had been keeping him alive ever since his body had started to fall apart.

Instinct.

Pure, stubborn instinct was all he had since his spirit had already been broken beyond all repair.

With his finger tightening on the trigger, Darrow could hear the first sound of the deputy's cry coming from the back of the kid's throat. Rather than take his point-blank shot, he shifted all of his weight to one side, forcing the deputy on the other side of the bars to move in the opposite direction.

The sickly prisoner wasn't able to do more than tilt the lawman slightly off-balance, but that was all he needed to put the kid between himself and the freshly drawn pistol of the second deputy. Using the deputy to keep him from falling completely backward, Darrow hung back and turned his head away as two gunshots were fired in quick succession.

Even though he could see what the prisoner was trying to do, the second deputy had already cleared leather and was taking his shot. Before his muscles had a chance to respond to the urgent demands from his brain, the hammer of the deputy's pistol had already dropped and the gun bucked against the palm of his hand.

The first round drilled into the side of the deputy who seemed to be stuck to the bars of the cell like glue. Because the lawman with the pistol had tried to divert his aim, the second shot went more to the side. This, however, only punched a hole through the lung of the kid Darrow was using as a human shield.

From the other side of the twitching body, Darrow opened his eyes and watched as all the life drained out of the kid, his mouth hung open with a final, unspoken plea. As always, when Darrow looked into the eyes of the dying, he couldn't help but feel a pang of jealousy. Then again, he also couldn't force back the instinct that fought to keep him from becoming a corpse himself.

Because of the narrow spaces between the bars, Darrow couldn't move his hand too much from side to side. Since the deputy's body was already starting to fall over, he pushed it as much as he could in that direction while stepping over to peek out from the other side.

Darrow wound up looking over the left shoulder of the dying man. His eyes met the panicked gaze of the second deputy who seemed to be in shock after seeing what he'd just done. That look of shock was frozen on the deputy's face, marred only when Darrow squeezed his trigger and knocked a third eye into the deputy's forehead.

The first deputy hit the floor and crumpled up like a worm that had been in the sun for too long. A quiet groan came from his throat, but it quickly faded away. The second deputy was still rocking back and forth on his feet, his arms twitching slightly but unable to hold up his gun.

Darrow took one look at the lawman who was still standing and quickly dismissed him, turning his attention instead to the one that was still within his reach.

"Jesus," Jasper whispered once he finally screwed up the courage to look up from where he'd been huddled. The moment he glanced at the bloody hallway outside the cells, his face went paler than Darrow's and his stomach started to convulse. "Jesus, God almighty!"

"Shut up," Darrow hissed. "And keep your supper down where it belongs or I'll shoot you myself."

"What . . . what have you done?"

"I'm getting us out of here."

"But they'll be coming." Panic was already bubbling up in the fat man's voice. "The rest of 'em will be coming and they'll shoot us both down. God and Jesus Christ!"

Darrow had been rummaging through the closest deputy's pockets through the bars. He smirked and pulled his hand out of the kid's shirt pocket, producing a ring of metal keys. One look was all he needed to form an opinion. "Shit!" He spat. "God dammit all to hell!"

The keys hung from a ring dangling from Darrow's finger. Not one of them were anywhere close to big enough to fit in the cell door's lock.

THIRTY

Clint left The Tweed House with a full belly and a couple minutes' rest to calm his nerves. He wasn't shaken up so much by the blood he'd seen spilled outside that bank, as he was by the look he'd gotten at the killer who'd pulled the trigger.

Although it had only been for a brief moment, the glimpse he'd gotten of Ellis Darrow was more than enough to send a chill down his spine. Clint was a man who lived by the gun and stayed alive a hell of a lot longer than most men who did the same thing. There were plenty of reasons for that, but the one that he was most aware of was his instinct to survive.

That instinct told him when he needed to play things safe and when he needed to put everything on the line. That instinct also told him when he could afford to rest and when he needed to move. It was that instinct that was screaming to him as soon as he walked out of Maribeth's saloon. And it was that instinct that put the glimpse of Ellis Darrow back into the front of his mind.

When Clint thought back to the killer's face, the one thing he focused on was his eyes. The eyes told a lot about any person as long as you knew how to read all the things you saw when looking into them. But Darrow's eyes were different. They were different simply because there was so little going on inside of them.

Even an animal had some emotions or intent reflected in the way they looked at someone. But Darrow's were as cold as two chunks of stone that had been set into his skull. They seemed even colder when Clint took into account that Darrow had been fresh out of killing three people when he'd been taken in by the sheriff. And by all accounts, there were only three dead because Darrow had been stopped before he could fire again.

Clint had been there. He'd seen the killer in his element and that was the only time he'd seen any spark of life in those eyes. Darrow looked like he was savoring every moment when he had that gun in his hand and it was that memory that caused Clint to break into a jog when he hit the street.

It wasn't that he had any particular mistrust of the sheriff or any lack of faith in his methods, but Clint just knew he had to get moving. That coldness in Darrow's eyes had been eating away at him ever since he'd first seen it and it wasn't until just now that he knew why.

Darrow was a walking dead man. Clint had seen the type only a few times in his lifetime, but he remembered every single one. The one that stuck out the most was Doc Holliday.

Eaten away from the inside by consumption, Holliday lived his life as though each day was his last. He gambled, drank, even fought knowing that he didn't have a damn thing to lose since he was already living on borrowed time. In that mind-set, Holliday figured he'd already lost so he might as well not hold back in anything he did.

There had been others that Clint remembered. Other men who were sick or injured or just so tired of living for whatever reason that dying didn't seem so bad. Those types were unpredictable and dangerous. Quite simply, they didn't act the way normal men acted.

A lot of the way Clint read other people had been learned from years of playing poker. That game was the perfect teacher in gauging others and even predicting what they might do next. Men like Holliday and Darrow didn't play by the same rules. They played as if every card they held was wild and raised the stakes accordingly.

All of this flew through Clint's mind as he raced down the street at an even quicker pace. By the time he could see the sheriff's office down the street, Clint was almost at a full run.

He knew there wasn't much time. Because men like Darrow and Holliday thought the way they did, they didn't take kindly to being locked in a cage. After all, when every moment could be their last, it only made sense that they wouldn't want to spend it in jail.

If anyone else had been locked away less than a few hours ago, they might sit tight for a while and wait for a good opportunity to arise before making a move. Hell, if any normal person was in that cell, they would more than likely eat their meals and sleep on their cot until they got their trial.

But Clint knew Darrow wasn't a normal person. He was going to do something, and he wouldn't wait long before doing it. The only thing that stuck in Clint's craw was that he hadn't thought about all of this sooner.

As if to remind him of all he'd been through in this single day, Clint felt his muscles start to ache and his head swim with the need for sleep. He found it nearly impossible to believe that at least four or five days hadn't passed since he'd taken his meal at Jesse's a few streets over. It felt more like a week had passed, but it hadn't even been a day.

Maybe that's what it felt like to walk around in Darrow's boots. In fact, at that very moment, Clint suddenly realized exactly why men like Darrow and Holliday lived the way they did.

Every moment did feel like it dragged by if it was packed to busting with constant activity and risk. Every day did feel like a week when it was spent without hardly a moment's rest.

Clint could afford to rest.

Dying men couldn't.

It was that simple.

Suddenly, Clint didn't feel bad at all for taking time to come to this realization. He might as well have expected to instantly know what it felt like to be an old fellow from the days of the Roman Empire. Those soldiers were separated from Clint by as much time as he was separated from Darrow by circumstance.

Now that he had some degree of understanding, Clint felt like he had a better handle on the situation. He was climbing the steps to the sheriff's office when he spotted something moving from the corner of his eye. One step away from entering the office, Clint saw Sheriff Anderson himself emerging from the alley next to the building.

Before he could say a thing to the lawman, Clint saw someone else opening the door directly in front of him. His eyes snapped over to the door and instead of seeing a deputy come from the office, he saw an attractive brunette staring back at him.

THIRTY-ONE

Their eyes met and Clint instantly remembered her as the
woman who'd been walking next to Darrow when they
were leaving the doctor's office earlier that night.

She must have recognized him as well because she
came out, took a few steps away from the door and started
running down the broadwalk.

Clint's first instinct was to grab her as she passed by
him. His arm snapped out immediately, but only got
a hold of her sleeve and a portion of her wrist. Anchoring
his feet, Clint leaned back and pulled as though he was a
fisherman hauling back on a line that had suddenly gone
taut.

Behind him, he could hear heavy footsteps thumping
against wooden planks. The walk bounced slightly beneath his feet as the sheriff came running up at full speed.

"Whoa there, Clint," Anderson said. "What's your
problem with her?"

Clint felt the lawman's hand drop onto his shoulder as
he tried to get a better grip on the brunette's wrist. She
was twisting and pulling away from him, tugging desper-
ately to get herself free.

"Whatever it is, you must be mistaken," the sheriff said

in a rush. "Can't you see you're scaring this poor girl?"

But Clint wasn't of a mind to explain himself right that moment. Instead, his main concern was keeping that woman from getting away until he could ask her a question or two. Also, he wasn't ready to leave the sheriff's office until he'd gotten a chance to look inside.

The more Ann twisted and pulled, the more of her wrist came out from between Clint's fingers. She gritted her teeth and put all of her strength into one last tug, which sent a painful jolt through her arm as Clint's grip tightened around the middle of her wrist.

Just when Clint thought he might be able to keep hold of her, he realized that he mostly had a hold of material instead of flesh and bone. After allowing herself to be pulled toward him an inch or two, she hauled back and wrenched herself away, leaving Clint with nothing but a fistful of material as her sleeve ripped off in his hand.

Clint's momentum sent him staggering back a couple steps as Ann bolted forward like a racehorse coming out of the gate. Before he had a chance to catch himself, Clint backed into a solid mass which allowed him to regain his footing. That solid mass was Sheriff Anderson, and he took hold of Clint's other shoulder to spin him around like a child.

"What in the blue hell was that all about?" the sheriff demanded.

Clint had already broken free of the lawman's grasp and threw the shredded dress sleeve to the ground. He didn't bother answering Anderson's question until he'd shouldered through the door to the sheriff's office and charged inside.

The burly lawman was right behind him, working himself up into more of a lather with each passing second. "I'm talking to you, Adams! God dammit, you'd better answer me!"

"That woman was with him," Clint said as he quickly looked around the inside of the office.

If he'd been looking at the sheriff's face, there would have been no way Clint could have missed the guilty look that suddenly appeared there.

"With who?" the sheriff asked.

"That killer in your jail. She was with him earlier today and she just came out of here now. Where the hell are your jail cells?"

"The jailhouse is one building away and what do you mean she's with that killer? She couldn't have been, since she was . . ." The sheriff let that statement trail off when he saw Clint start rummaging around the desk and cabinets at the back of the room. "What are you doing?"

Wheeling around to look at the lawman for the first time since before he'd charged into the room, Clint said, "She was in here for a reason. Look around and tell me if anything is missing . . . anything important like weapons or—"

"Keys." Anderson didn't say that as though he was trying to finish Clint's statement. Instead, he was speaking as though he'd said the word more to himself.

Clint followed the lawman's gaze to an empty hook on the wall next to a gun cabinet. He was already heading for the door when he asked, "Those were keys to the jail cells, right?"

"Dammit!"

That was close enough to a yes for Clint's purposes. He didn't wait around for the sheriff to say another word before he was out the door and running along the boardwalk. He could hear those heavy footsteps following closely behind him.

"This way," Anderson said as he caught up to Clint. "The new jailhouse wasn't here the last time you were in town."

Clint watched the other man turn a corner and head for

a building that had been built in what used to be a vacant lot behind the sheriff's office the last time Clint had seen it. The front door was open and the woman's silhouette could be seen heading inside.

Both men were already running as fast as they could when the sound of gunfire thundered from the building in front of them. Pouring out every last bit of energy he could muster, Clint felt his legs start to burn as he pushed himself to go even faster toward the building.

"How many deputies were watching the prisoners?" Clint shouted over his shoulder.

The sheriff's breathing sounded like a powerful engine as he kept pace with Clint. "Two. There was supposed to be one in the office and the rest were making their rounds."

"Go get them. I'll see what's going on inside and try to keep it from spilling out onto the street."

"No way, Adams. I'm not about to let you go against that animal on your own. I don't care who you are."

They slowed their pace rather than burst into the jailhouse blindly at full speed. Clint's hand was closed around the grip of his Colt and he didn't take his eyes away from the jailhouse's front door. "You know where to find your men, Sheriff. I don't. Put them on alert so they can keep anyone else from getting hurt. There's no more time to bicker."

Sheriff Anderson wanted to protest, but he knew that Clint was right. Besides, there was no one left to argue with since Clint had already ducked inside the jailhouse.

THIRTY-TWO

When Darrow heard the footsteps racing through the hall-way, he pressed his face against the bars so he could get a look at who was coming. The pistol he'd taken moved to point in his direct line of sight as though it had already become a part of his own body.

"Ellis!" Ann yelled when she saw his hand poking out from between the bars. "They're coming right behind me. Here."

She didn't know for sure what cell he was in, but any question along that line was answered when she saw the bodies of the deputies lying in front of one of the barred doors. The pistol was the next thing to catch her attention, which was what she aimed for when tossing the ring of keys down the hall.

Darrow shot his free hand through the bars just in time to snatch the keys from the air. "You see, Jasper," he said while fitting the first key he could single out into the lock. "This is why you need to get yourself a good woman." That key didn't fit, so he went to the next one in line. "They may have their faults, but a good woman will be there when you need her."

If the fat man heard a word Darrow was saying, he

didn't give the first indication. Jasper was too busy pushing himself back farther against the rear wall of his cell and pressing the palms of his hands against his ears.

Darrow didn't give a damn if he was being heard or not. Every one of his senses were already focused in on more than enough already. His hands felt for the keyhole as he fit another key into place. When that one didn't move inside the lock, he slid it out and moved on.

His ears were straining to hear the steps of those others that Ann had been talking about and his eyes were looking for another figure nearby besides the approaching woman running toward his cell. He caught a glimpse of just such a figure when he fit the next key into his door. Without a moment's hesitation, Darrow shifted the pistol in his hand and pulled the trigger.

Ann ducked her head slightly, but kept running toward Darrow. She was close enough to see the sliver of his face that could make it between the bars and smiled at him even as bullets whipped past her head.

"Step aside, darling," was all Darrow said before he pulled his trigger again.

Accustomed to following such orders instantly, Ann threw herself against the barred doors opposite Darrow's cell as he fired another shot through the place she'd just been standing. Every time the gun in Darrow's hand roared, Ann felt a tingling sensation pass through her body. Lacing her fingers in between the bars behind her back, she pulled in a quick breath and watched Darrow take another shot.

With one hand still on the key protruding from the lock on his door, Darrow tossed the deputy's pistol to the floor and held that hand open. "There should be another one of those on the floor by your feet," he said to Ann without looking at her. "Find it and hand it over, will you?"

Ann dropped to her knees and ran her hands over the deputy's body, starting near the holster strapped to his side. "It's the sheriff," she said while going through her motions. "Him and some other man were on their way over, but I got past them both and made it here."

The other figure at the end of the hall had ducked out of sight for the moment, which allowed Darrow to take his eyes from that end of the hall and glance over toward Ann. "I'll bet that other man was tall and had a scar running down one side of his face."

Her eyes widened just before looking down to search for the gun. "That's right. He was almost quick enough to stop me, but I got past him."

"That'd be Clint Adams."

"Clint Adams? Is he—"

"Yes, darling. He is. Now try by his hand instead. Hurry it up now."

It took a moment for her to realize that the last part of that statement was referring to the deputy and not the Gunsmith. She found the outstretched hand Darrow had been referring to and quickly spotted the pistol lying close by on the floor. Her hands closed around the weapon, sending another pleasurable jolt through her skin which only grew when she handed the gun to Darrow.

After a moment's calculation in his head, Darrow figured how many shots should be in the weapon and pointed it toward the other end of the hall. From there, he took hold of the key in the lock and gave it a try. It twisted in place, letting out a satisfying clank once the door was unlocked.

"Looks like I've got two lovely ladies on my side tonight," the killer said while kicking open the door.

Before he could take two steps, Darrow was nearly knocked back into his cell when Ann came rushing toward him. He'd been expecting her to do exactly that, so he was ready to catch her when she threw open her arms and pressed herself against his sunken chest.

"I tried to give you enough time," she said in words

that were muffled since her face was buried in his shirt. "I didn't want to let you down."

"Let me down? Hardly." Without letting the pistol in his hand waver from its target, Darrow slid the fingers of his free hand through Ann's thick, black hair and pulled her close enough to give her a deep, passionate kiss.

"What about me?" Jasper asked from the rear corner of his own cell. "Are you gonna let me out of here?"

"You gonna pay me the money you owe me?" Darrow asked.

The fat man started to put together a lie in his head, but couldn't get his tongue to form the words correctly. No matter how much it pained him, the truth was the only thing that could slide from his mouth at that point in time. "I don't have the money. Not since we got caught. This went all wrong," he added, turning angry and flushing red. "That wasn't part of the deal."

Shrugging, Darrow said, "That's right. But neither was this."

The pistol in Darrow's hand snapped around until Jasper was staring down its barrel. The expression on the sickly man's face didn't shift in the slightest with the decision to end Jasper's life. Instead, the skin around his eyes only pinched in a bit and his tongue flicked out to wet his cracked bottom lip.

Ann's face reflected enough expression for the both of them. When she looked over to Jasper, her mouth opened slightly and her breast swelled with a sudden intake of air.

"Not again," came a voice from the opposite end of the hall. "Not this time."

Ann looked toward the sound of that voice and tightened her grip around Darrow's slender body. What she saw was a figure that nearly filled up the entire doorway. There was nothing but darkness behind him, but Clint's face was illuminated by the flickering light of the lanterns hanging from the jailhouse's rafters.

Neither Darrow nor Jasper took their eyes off of each other. One man was too concerned with saving his life, and the other seemed consumed by the act of taking it away.

Clint took a few steps forward, which was just enough for the light to shine upon the Colt in his hand. "You kill that man and I'll be forced to gun you down where you stand," he said. "I may not know you, but I know you don't want to die like that."

Hearing those words was enough to shift the expression on Darrow's face. It wasn't much more than a subtle tilt of his head and a narrowing of his eyes, but it was enough for Jasper to notice. Suddenly, Darrow didn't seem so cold and detached.

He didn't look afraid, either.

He did, however, look interested in what Clint was saying.

THIRTY-THREE

Any other time when he knew he had to work quickly or risk letting a killer get away, Clint would have been willing to gamble with his own life by charging into a place like that jailhouse. But this wasn't a situation like any other. He'd figured out that much before walking up to the door, which was still ajar after Ann had run through it.

If he charged into the jailhouse, he might just get Darrow to kill someone else out of reflex. Having heard the gunshots before, Clint was fairly certain that someone else was already hurt, but he couldn't do anything about that just then. All he could do was his best to make sure that the casualties were kept to a minimum.

Unfortunately, with a man like Ellis Darrow, that minimum would probably still be awful high.

Clint made his way to the door and pressed his back against the wall right next to it. The Colt was in his hand and ready as he took a peek around the door frame at what was going on inside the jail. He could tell right away that the woman was rushing to bring the keys to Darrow. He could also tell that the sickly man was armed and ready to shoot.

The deputies' bodies were plain enough to see and Clint had to fight to keep himself from rushing inside when he thought there was a chance either one of the lawmen might still be alive. Neither of them moved, even as Ann rummaged through one of their pockets.

Wanting to get a look at how Darrow would operate under such tense circumstances, Clint watched as he got the keys and started trying to unlock the door. He was glad he'd held back on running into the jail when Darrow's eyes snapped over to lock on to him and a shot came soon after.

The bullet took a chunk from the door frame, which considering how little Darrow could have seen of his target, was still impressive. Clint tried to keep his eyes on the killer, but a couple more shots in his direction had forced him to pull back around the corner.

It wasn't until Clint heard Jasper begging for his life that he knew he had to make his play. Even if it was a slimy toad like Jasper Prescott, Clint wasn't about to let someone else die if he could help it. He stepped into the doorway and said his piece, not bothering to try and predict what Darrow might do in return.

The killer might decide to test his mettle against Clint or he might try to get out through a back door that Clint wasn't aware of. Then again, he might put a bullet through Jasper's skull just for the hell of it. All Clint knew for sure was that the sickly gunman seemed to be listening to him when the conversation had turned toward the subject of death.

"And what would you know about how I want to die?" Darrow asked. "You don't know a goddamn thing about me."

"Sure I do. For example, I know you don't just have a death wish or you would have caught a bullet a long time ago. And you're no mad-dog killer, or you would have put that sorry sack of dung out of his misery way before now."

That brought a smile to Darrow's face. "I still might. You think the world would miss another fat pig like this sucking down all its air and choking down all its food?"

"Probably not," Clint said with a shrug. "And I'm not here to tell you any different."

"Then why are you here, Gunsmith?"

"To see that justice is done."

"Is that all?"

"No. I also need to make sure you stay in that cage of yours until you stand in front of a judge. I can't have you walking around free," Clint said frankly. "Not after what you've done."

Darrow nodded and looked at Jasper and then to Ann. "You're not a bullshitter, Adams. I like that about you. That's a rare thing to find in someone these days."

As he'd been talking, Clint had taken a few slow, cautious steps down the hall. He hadn't covered much more than a few feet of ground, but it was closer than he'd been before. Every step he took felt like a step into uncharted territory. It still might have caused Darrow to do any number of things. Or, it could bring about nothing at all.

The uncertainty was starting to get under Clint's skin, but he wasn't about to let it force him into doing anything before he was ready.

Mainly, the reason he'd taken those steps forward was not to crowd Darrow or even close the gap between them in case he needed to gun the killer down. He could just as easily have put a bullet into him from outside the jail as he could from two feet through the door. What he wanted to do was keep the doorway clear for when Sheriff Anderson came back with the rest of his deputies.

Judging by the sound of boots against the dirt and hushed voices drawing closer, the lawmen would be bursting through the door any second.

"So what now, Adams?" Darrow asked. The woman beside him was getting anxious, but she kept quiet and still since she had yet to get any indication that Darrow wanted her to do otherwise. "Are you willing to shoot at me to save this pig and risk hitting this young lady, here?"

"That's no risk for me," Clint said. "I think you already know that."

"Yeah," That word came out of Darrow's mouth like the last breath from a dying man. "I know all about you."

Even from where he was standing, Clint could see the conflict flooding through Darrow's eyes. But since he could barely comprehend what might be going through someone like Darrow's mind, Clint didn't even try to read the things he saw reflected in those bloodshot pupils.

Suddenly, the jailhouse filled with the thunderous racket of heavy footsteps pounding over the floorboards as Sheriff Anderson charged inside like he was leading the Cavalry. Clint's body tensed, waiting to see if the appearance of all those lawmen would be enough to push Darrow into a bloody frenzy.

But the killer hardly moved. In fact, he let the pistol dangle from his trigger finger and held his hands up over his head.

THIRTY-FOUR

Clint went right along with the sheriff and his men as they carefully approached Darrow. As the killer's wrists and ankles were bound in chains, Clint stood at the ready in case either Darrow or his woman were going to try anything.

Ann looked as if she was keeping just as ready as Clint, but something was holding her back. Every so often she would look over to the sickly man and when she didn't get a look in return, she kept still and finally let the deputies take her into their custody.

Throughout the entire process, Darrow kept his eyes on Clint. There was a moment of tension when the sheriff himself reached up to relieve Darrow of the pistol he'd taken from the deputy. Every one of Clint's muscles were waiting for Darrow to try and spin the pistol back into firing position and take one more shot at the lawmen. Not only did that shot never come, but Darrow seemed to enjoy the uneasiness he was creating.

It wasn't until the killer was chained and led to one of the cells closer to the back of the jailhouse that Sheriff Anderson allowed himself to look at the bodies on the floor. One of the younger men that had burst into the jail was in the process of searching Ann when the sheriff turned to look at the woman.

"What was your part in this?" he asked.

Clint was about to offer what he knew, but surprisingly enough the brunette didn't have any reservations about telling her own story.

"I took the keys from right under your nose," she said with a mocking smile. "And before that, I made sure you weren't around when those people in that bank really needed you."

Anderson replied to that comment with a backhand that was so swift, Clint didn't even get a chance to try and stop him. That would have been his first instinct since striking a woman was almost never justified in his eyes. Then again, after hearing what she had to say, Clint really couldn't blame Anderson for losing control for a moment.

"You goddamn whore," Anderson snarled.

Her face had snapped to one side when the sheriff's blow had landed. Now, Ann looked up at him and grinned as the younger deputy held on to her a little tighter. "Think back a moment," she said. "When you were supposed to be out doing your job, who was on their back grunting like a rutting dog? Think back and ask yourself if I'm really the only whore in this room."

Ann finished her insult with her chin sticking out as though she was daring the lawman to hit her again. The sheriff seemed more than ready to oblige, but when he pulled back his hand again, it was held in place by a sudden, firm grip.

"Let me go," Anderson said without even looking at who'd stopped him.

It was Clint's hand wrapped around the sheriff's wrist, and that hand didn't budge no matter how much fury was seeped in the lawman's voice. Instead, Clint held on until he felt some of the tension ease from Anderson's muscles. Only then did he relax his grip in the slightest.

"Back off, Sheriff," Clint said. "Your job isn't to beat the prisoners to a pulp."

"These aren't prisoners," he said. "They're animals. Look around you, Adams! These were my men he killed. And I knew those folks in the bank as well." The sheriff turned to look Clint in the eyes while tearing his hand free. To the deputies holding Ann by the arms, he said, "Take her to one of the old cells. I don't want her to even see that other one's face."

Reluctantly, the two younger men nodded and dragged her down the hall to the door, which still swung open on its hinges.

The sheriff watched them leave, but stopped them before they could get her outside. "Wait," he said. "Look at me, both of you." Like a father addressing two of his own sons, Anderson waited until he could see the whites of both the deputies' eyes. "I want her to make it to that cell alive and unhurt. Understand?"

The deputies paused and gritted their teeth to keep from saying what their boss just wanted to hear. Anderson's words somehow made it through everything else that was going on inside of them whether they wanted them to or not.

Nodding, first one and then the other replied, "Yes, sir."

When they turned back to the door and started walking again, the deputies treated Ann with slightly less roughness. They allowed her to try and walk with them rather than simply pulling her between them like she was already nothing more than dead weight.

The sheriff watched them go and let out a slow, troubled breath. "I should've killed them myself," he said in a voice that was barely loud enough to be heard by the man standing right next to him. "There isn't a man in this country that would have held me accountable after what happened here tonight. In fact, there's plenty that would've considered it a service. Most would've considered it my duty."

"True," Clint answered. "But what do you think kept you from doing it? Surely you don't consider my counsel over everything else?"

"No. Although it was you that kept that . . . thing . . . in the cell down there alive. And you also had something to do with keeping them boys from harming that filthy whore of a woman."

Clint waited for the sheriff to finish what he was saying. After a few seconds, the sound of something scraping along the jail's floors filled the air like a sack of grain being dragged behind a cart. Both Clint and the sheriff looked in that direction and saw Jasper crawling out of his corner and pulling himself up onto his cot. The door of the farthest cell down the row slammed shut and the noisy rattle of the lock echoed through the barred hallway.

Hearing those things seemed to pull Anderson out of whatever he'd been thinking like a spray of cold water in his face. He turned to look at Clint, looking not quite his normal self, but more like the lawman that Clint remembered.

"You've got some talking to do, Adams," the sheriff said. "But not here. Come with me."

By the tone in the lawman's voice alone, Clint felt compelled to follow as Anderson started walking toward the front door.

THIRTY-FIVE

Although only a few minutes had passed since the last time he'd been outside, Clint swore that the temperature had dropped twenty degrees. Montana nights in autumn were known to get chilly, but the bite in the air came from a lot more than just cold.

The sheriff's disposition was a factor, but only a small one. Mainly, the cold came from inside Clint's own chest. If he took a moment to allow memories of what had happened to float through his mind, Clint felt himself get even colder.

"Start talking," Anderson said.

Clint pulled in a lungful of crisp air, which helped to clear his mind somewhat. "All right. Where should I start?"

"Well, you can start with why you feel the need to keep that piece-of-shit killer alive in there when it would have been so much easier to put him in the ground where he belongs?"

"Easier?"

"Yeah. That's what I said. It would have been a hell of a lot easier than putting him up and feeding him for a couple more days until he goes to trial, wastes a judge's

time, and then gets his neck stretched at the end of a
noose."

The sheriff was about the same size as Clint, except
with a bit more meat on his bones. He looked like a man
who'd been through a lot and was all the tougher for it.
His skin was leathery and coarse and he was an even more
imposing sight when he put both hands on his hips and
squared his shoulders with Clint's.

Standing tall without trying to assert himself, Clint held
the sheriff's gaze and didn't flinch when the other man
barked his words directly into his face.

"You're right, Sheriff," Clint said. "That would have
been a whole lot easier and I wouldn't presume to tell you
your job."

"That's funny because you seem to be presuming a
whole lot around here."

"Maybe you needed a little reminder, that's all."

Anderson's eyes narrowed and he spoke through a
clenched jaw. "Is that a fact? And what did I need to be
reminded of by the likes of you?"

"That you're the sheriff of this town and not its executioner."

Those words had a definite effect upon the big lawman.
They soaked through all the anger and frustration just as
his own words had gotten through to his deputies.

As if reading that same notion from the sheriff's head,
Clint paused a moment and then asked, "Why did you
stop those men of yours from doing what you know they
were going to do to that woman once they got her alone?"

Anderson shook his head slowly. "The hell if I know."

"Sure you do. You stopped them because no matter
how much they wanted to tear her apart and no matter
how much it might have been justified, that simply wasn't
the right thing to do."

"But I'm supposed to be the justice in this town."

"And you're also supposed to lead by example. Isn't

that why a sheriff is supposed to be a good member of his community and follow all the rules he enforces? It's not all a show and you know that every bit as much as I do."

"Yeah. I know." Anderson turned away from Clint and stretched his back. Looking up at the clear night sky, he seemed to lose himself among the millions of twinkling lights over his head. It was only a few seconds later when he rubbed his hands over his face and said, "All right, Adams. Now that you got to ask your questions, how about answering some of mine?"

Clint was looking up at the stars as well. On a night like the one he'd had, it was all too easy to let his mind become preoccupied with the simple task of making invisible pictures by connecting the celestial dots. He didn't take his eyes from the heavens as he said, "I'll do my best, but I can't make any promises."

"Fair enough." Digging into his shirt pocket, the lawman fished out a half-burned stub of a cigar and stuck it in his mouth. He found a match next, struck it against the side of the jailhouse and ignited the end of the cigar until it was glowing brightly. Letting a cloud of acrid smoke flow from between his lips, he said, "You've killed plenty of men. In fact, I know you've killed plenty of men that have done a lot less than the one in that cell."

At that moment, hearing those words wasn't easy, but Clint couldn't exactly refute them either. Instead, he nodded and let his eyes keep moving from one star to another.

"And since you're not a lawman," Anderson continued, "why didn't you kill him?" He paused for a second, waiting for an answer. When he saw one wasn't directly on its way, he said, "You were there at the bank. You saw what he did. He even talked to you for a bit, didn't he?"

Clint nodded. "Yeah. He said some things."

"You were here too. You saw what he did to my men and what he was about to do. He even tried putting a bullet into you on both of those occasions."

"Yep. More than one bullet, actually."

"Then answer my question. Why didn't you kill him?"

"Because, no matter what that outlaw or anyone else thinks about me, I'm not a killer. I do what I have to do when I have to do it. Sometimes, I have to kill and other times I don't. I was never too comfortable with going against my gut instincts because when it comes to life and death, that's the only thing I listen to. Anything else would be me making judgments I'm not qualified to make."

Anderson took the cigar out of his mouth and spit a piece of tobacco onto the ground. "If you're not qualified to decide a murdering bastard like Ellis Darrow, then who the hell is?"

Clint looked at the sheriff just long enough to direct the lawman's eyes back up to the stars. A simple point toward the sky was all that was needed to answer Anderson's question.

"I never thought of you as a religious man," Anderson said.

"I never did either. But that's the best answer I can come up with right now."

"That's what came from your gut, you mean?"

Smiling slightly, Clint nodded. "Yeah. I guess it is."

THIRTY-SIX

"Well as fascinating as that subject may be, I'm not exactly the man to discuss it with you. We do have a preacher in town who would love to bend your ear on them kind of mysteries. I do still have a matter to discuss with you that's a little more my speed."

"What's that, Sheriff?"

"Well, since neither of us has the sand to put that killer on the first train to Hades, then I need to figure out what to do with him. I know he needs to stand trial, and I sure as hell know he needs to hang. But you're either a damn good judge of character or you're having a real lucky day because I know I'm not the man to perform either of them two services."

Clint rubbed the back of his neck, which had become sore after looking up for so long. "It's got nothing to do with any of those things, Sheriff. I've worked with you before, if you remember, and I know that you tend to do things the right way whenever you can. If you were the bloodthirsty type, those outlaws who were in this town could have been picked off by a rifle from a rooftop or shot in their sleep."

Letting out a heavy sigh at those particular memories,

Anderson said, "There's plenty in town who think that's exactly what I should have done."

"If you were a hired killer or vigilante, then yeah. That was what you should have done. But you're a lawman." Clint had formed his opinion regarding Anderson's competence the first time he was in town, and it hadn't changed. Rather than go into that subject, however, he said, "Sometimes that's easier than others, but you stuck to your guns. That's a good thing."

"If you say so. What I'm trying to say is that although I'm not about to hold a trial or string that asshole up, both of those things need to be done as soon as possible."

"I agree with that."

"Judge Dodd won't be coming through these parts for another two weeks. And after what happened here tonight, I'm not too happy with the notion of keeping Darrow here for one more night if I can help it. I may be a lawman down to the core, but me and my deputies are only human. If we have to look at that bastard's face too many times, one of us will put a bullet through it."

"That's understandable. So, what are you driving at?"

"I'm offering you a job, Adams. It shouldn't take you long and you'll get paid your due. I've got no way to force you into anything, since God knows you've done plenty for us already."

Glancing back into the jailhouse, Clint caught a glimpse of the deputies that had taken up their spots directly in front of Darrow's cell. "Some might say that not all I've done recently was too good."

"I doubt it, but if there's any cross words out there for you, don't listen to a damn single one of them." The sheriff reached out to pat Clint on the shoulder. For a man who barely let his guard down over the course of his entire life, the simple gesture spoke volumes. "I've never heard anything but praise about you, Adams. In fact, that's something that's been stuck in my craw since the day you left the first time.

"And if I ever did hear anything like that, I'd knock out whoever said it." This time, Anderson also looked into the jailhouse and saw one of his men glance back at him. "That goes the same no matter who says it. Even if it's one of my own boys."

Clint hadn't been bothered by what the deputies might have thought about him until he'd just now seen how they looked at him when they thought he couldn't see them. It wasn't so much that he held the opinion of others in such high regard, but those subtle glances hit upon a nerve that had already been torn open inside of Clint's chest. It was the part of him that wanted nothing more than to go against what his gut instinct was telling him, no matter how right or wrong it might have been.

"Thanks, Sheriff. I appreciate that."

"Well, don't thank me yet. Not until you hear about the job I'm offering."

"I'm listening."

"I've had enough folks killed in my town and besides that, I'm sick of looking at that asshole's grinning face. I want him to face his music and I want him the hell out of Broken Cross. Judge Dodd won't be here for a while, but he'll be in Winston for the next ten days or so."

"And you want me to take him," Clint said more as a statement of fact than a question.

Anderson nodded once and took another drag from his cigar. "That's right. I'd do it myself, but I can't exactly pick up and leave this town after all that's happened. Nothing against my deputies, but none of them have ever really dealt with a killer like that one.

"Besides, getting Darrow away from town and out on the trail would test the limits of any man. I doubt he'd make it to his trial before either escaping or getting his head blown off by one of my boys." He took another puff and shrugged. "Or even by me, for that matter."

"So you think I'm the only one who can resist shooting Darrow?"

"Hell yes. Especially since you've already proved it twice now."

Clint couldn't help but laugh. "Considering all the stories going around about me, I find that observation of yours to be pretty damn ironic."

Sheriff Anderson thought about it as he rolled some smoke around in his mouth. Before long, he was laughing as well, his wide shoulders shaking up and down as he chomped on the cigar. "Well, ironic or not, that's the job. You feel like taking it?"

"How far is it to Winston?"

"No more than a four or five day ride. Maybe three if you put the spurs to your ride and haul ass through part of the night."

"And what about the woman?"

"We can hold on to her without too much problem. I have a feeling that most of the fight will be out of her once she sees her man get taken out of town. Besides, my boys may be angry but they're not about to go killing a woman."

Clint kept his eyes on the lawman for a couple seconds. "That's your boys, but what about you? Something tells me that you and the woman have something going on between you. Maybe some unfinished business that some time with just you and her inside a cell could fix?"

The hint of a smile was still on Anderson's face when he asked, "Did you figure that all out on your own or did you just happen to listen to what she was saying when she was screaming loud enough to wake the dead?"

"A little bit of both, perhaps."

"She came to me before the bank was hit. I'm sure you know what I'm saying when I talk about the kind of woman who wants to get her hands on a man with a reputation, even if it's just for one night. Maybe give herself something to make her own self feel wilder than she was before."

"I've known a woman like that or two in my time."

"I'll bet," Anderson said with a knowing smirk. "Well she came on like one of those, all hands and legs making it clear that she wanted to get me alone. I didn't have much against that, but she was just trying to keep me away from where I needed to be. The short of it is that she did her job and I didn't do mine. End of story."

"I'd give you advice on when to trust women, Sheriff, but first I'd have to find a man who knew a damn thing about the matter."

For the next couple of seconds, Clint and the sheriff tried to put some distance between themselves and the blood that had filled the day behind them. Unfortunately, a few seconds was all either of them could manage.

"About that job," Clint said. "I'll take it. Mind if I head out in the morning so I can get some rest?"

"Not at all. In fact, I'd insist. Gunsmith or not, if you're escorting the likes of Ellis Darrow, you'll need all the rest you can get."

THIRTY-SEVEN

Although Clint had been planning on getting a room at the hotel with the fancy sign at the end of Mill Street, he found himself instead walking back to The Tweed House. The saloon was doing a fair amount of business, but seemed to keep all the drinkers and gamblers under control no matter how many of them were packed inside the room.

That feat was pulled off by the solitary woman who stood upon the stage wearing a purple dress and matching satin gloves. She sang a slow, heartfelt number that was accompanied only by piano. Her voice soothed all the rowdy beasts and drew the attention of all but the most focused card players.

Even Clint felt his nerves loosen up a bit as he stepped into the place and stopped to listen to a few of the singer's verses. Before too long, he felt a hand on his shoulder and saw Maribeth Tweed sidle up next to him.

"She's good, isn't she?" Maribeth asked.

"Anyone that could take my shoulders from down around my ears deserves a medal."

"Awwww, poor baby." Saying that, Maribeth moved behind Clint and used both hands to massage his shoulders. She started close to the base of his neck and slowly worked her way down to just above his elbows.

As Maribeth's hands kneaded his muscles, Clint felt his head start to loll forward and his eyelids become heavy. She read his body like an open book and moved her hands to a spot between his shoulder blades, working them down along his spine.

"No need to hand over that medal just yet," she whispered into his ear. "You can send it to me later."

"Don't think that I won't. Damn, that feels good."

"You look dead on your feet, Clint. I could have someone arrange for a room at the Three Star if you like."

"I was headed there, but I thought I could come here instead."

"You need a drink?"

"Actually, I was hoping to spend the night on that bed of yours upstairs. I haven't felt anything that comfortable beneath me since . . . well . . . since you've been beneath me."

Maribeth's lips curled into a wide, genuinely happy smile. "You sure know how to charm a girl, Clint Adams. As good as that line was, it wasn't necessary. I'd let you get up on that stage and try to dance before I let you sleep anywhere but in that bed with me."

That was all Clint needed to hear. Actually, that was all Clint had wanted to hear. Everything after that was small talk and idle conversation as they worked their way through the saloon and headed for the door at the back of the room. They walked down the familiar hallway and Maribeth stopped before climbing the stairs.

"You go on up," she said. "Make yourself comfortable. You know where everything is."

"What about you?"

"I just need to tend to a few things. You know, just to make sure the place doesn't burn down or fall apart without me in sight for a little while. I'll also make arrangements to have breakfast waiting for you. How early were you planning on getting up?"

Clint shook his head. "Letting me use the room is enough. You don't have to get breakf—"

"Shut it," she snapped. "How early?"

"Pretty early."

"That's all I need to know." With that, Maribeth spun on the balls of her feet and headed back to the door which led to the saloon's main room. She was through the door before Clint could get another word out of his mouth.

He felt a little guilty for accepting the royal treatment from her like that, but he also knew it would have been useless to try and talk her out of it. So instead of fussing about it, Clint climbed the stairs and decided to just enjoy the comfortable bed as well as whatever breakfast Maribeth arranged for him.

Clint kicked off his boots as soon as he was inside her private bedroom. On the way to the bed, he shed his shirt and pants, sliding beneath the covers and into an almost instantaneous slumber. Of course, he didn't realize he'd fallen asleep until he felt the sheets move and the mattress shift beneath him.

He would have sworn that he'd just lay down and closed his eyes, but the cause of the movements in the bed was Maribeth crawling in beside him. She wore a soft, silk nightgown, which brushed against Clint's skin. The warmth of her body could be felt through the filmy material as she pressed herself against him and put one arm over his body.

"You were snoring," she said, confirming Clint's suspicion that more time had passed than what he'd thought.

Stretching and rolling onto his back, Clint took a deep breath and tried to focus his eyes in the darkness. "How long were you gone?"

"Less than an hour. I had to iron out a few scrapes downstairs and then see to your breakfast, but everything's under control. I hope none of the noise downstairs bothered you too much."

"No. Not at all." Some of the cobwebs were clearing out of Clint's mind. In fact, even with the little bit of sleep he'd gotten he was starting to feel better all around.

"So what happened with the sheriff?" Maribeth asked.

Without getting into too much detail, Clint gave her a rundown of what had happened. He started with the attempted breakout at the jail and told her about most of his conversation with Sheriff Anderson. He skipped over some of the parts that would have been embarrassing to the lawman, but by the look on Maribeth's face, she probably already had her own suspicions regarding that.

When he was finished with the story, Clint sat up and looked at Maribeth. His eyes had become adjusted to the dark and he could tell she was gazing thoughtfully back at him. "Did you hear about any of that through the rumor mill over here?"

"Of course. Not as much as what happened with the bank. Just that there were some gunshots coming from the jailhouse. Most folks thought Anderson or one of the deputies was giving that killer what he deserved."

Clint didn't have an answer for that. Instead he nodded and stared ahead into a thick clump of shadows.

Shifting so that she was lying on her side with her head resting on Clint's chest, Maribeth slipped one arm beneath his back and ran the other hand over his midsection. "Tell me something, Clint. Why didn't you shoot that man?"

"You mean Darrow?"

"You know who I mean. After all those times he tried to shoot you and after all those other people he killed, how come you didn't shoot him? Was it because of Anderson? With your reputation in this town, I doubt you could do much of anything to get on anyone's bad side."

"I told you about what I said to the sheriff," Clint answered. "And no matter how many times I shot Darrow, it wouldn't have brought a single one of those poor people back from the dead."

"I know that, and I'm not trying to say you did anything wrong. I'm just curious because it seems like you stopped yourself. There wasn't anything to be done about those people at the bank or even the deputies by the sound of it. But even when you could have been killed yourself, you kept from shooting him. Why was that?"

Clint thought for a moment. He didn't have to think about his reasoning, but he did have to come up with the words for what had been on his mind ever since he'd first seen that look in Darrow's eyes. Finally, he let out a breath and said, "I didn't shoot him because I think keeping him alive is the worst punishment I could give him."

THIRTY-EIGHT

Maribeth looked at him and even in the darkness, Clint could see the puzzled expression on her face. She started to respond to his answer a couple of times, but her words seemed to fail her. Finally, she laid her head back down on his chest.

"If you ask me, every one of those killer types wants to die," she said. "Why else would they put themselves in so many dangerous spots and keep getting themselves shot at all the time?"

"Sometimes, those dangerous spots seem to find you," Clint said off-handedly.

"So why not give him what he wants?" she asked. "That way, everybody is better off."

"Because it was something he said to me. He said that he knew what kind of man I was, and that he knew I wanted to kill him so bad I could taste it. Well, it was something like that anyway."

"Well that's just plain ridiculous. You may be good with a gun but you're not a killer, Clint. That's absurd."

"Is it?"

Those two words hung in the air like smoke from the sheriff's cigar. They drifted around and made the air harder to breathe. They even made Clint start to feel like he was being smothered.

"I've been thinking," Clint said after a while. "And I think he might not have been as crazy as he sounds. I did want to kill him, Maribeth. And there was a big part of me that wanted to kill him even after everything was said and done at the bank. When the law came busting in and the smoke was settling, there was a part of me that wanted to put my gun to that man's skull and pull the trigger."

"Don't get yourself worked up about that. Everyone in town wants that man dead. That only makes you human."

Clint shook his head and let his fingers wander through the strands of Maribeth's hair. "There's talk and there's truth. Most folks talk plenty about killing, but they've never done it and probably never will. I've killed people, Maribeth. Lots of people. There isn't a one of them I'd consider a murder, but dead is dead.

"Darrow looked at me and said I was a killer just like him. The proof was in what I was thinking when I pulled the trigger. At least, that's how I see it. I don't like seeing myself in that light."

Maribeth shifted beneath the sheets until she could climb on top of him and place both hands flat upon his chest. The nightgown was hanging off of one shoulder and her hair spilled down around her face. Her eyes stared straight down into his with so much intensity that they seemed like the brightest things inside that entire room.

"You listen to me, Clint Adams. You are not a killer." She touched his palms with her fingertips and said, "These are not a killer's hands. You fight for people who need your help and you only hurt those that are going to hurt others. Don't let some fast-talking devil make you think otherwise."

"I know all that," Clint said with the best smile he could manage. Even though the grin was somewhat weak, it did seem to put her at ease just a little. "I'm not a murderer, but I have killed and that makes me a killer. I know what Darrow was doing and I know what he wants more than anything else. Me not killing him is a way to prove him wrong and give him what he deserves.

"Some of what he said hit home and that makes me feel uneasy. But what still bothers me is how hard it is to keep myself from pulling the trigger when I'm in shooting distance of that animal. I did want to kill him and I still do. That bothers me."

"So why not just let Sheriff Anderson handle Darrow and be done with it?" she asked. "You've done your part. Hell, you've done so much more than your part. Hand all of this over to the ones that wear the badges. It's their job anyway."

"Too late for that. I've already accepted the job. Besides, Anderson has good reason to ask me for help on this."

"So what are you going to do once it's just you and Darrow out on the trail? Do you plan on working out your moral questions while he's trying to get free and put a bullet through your head?"

"Why? Does that sound like a bad plan to you?"

For a moment, Maribeth stared down at Clint with shock. It only took her a second or two to see the grin creeping across Clint's face. Once she saw that, she straightened up and smacked her hand lightly onto his side. "I'm being serious! What if you second-guess yourself at the wrong time and something happens to you?"

"I know better than that."

"Really? Because I'm starting to think that you've been surviving off of good luck and God's will up to now."

"Yeah? No experience or skill factors into it?"

"Nope. Not a bit."

"Then I truly am up a creek because I was hoping my lucky rabbit's foot would keep me alive when I'm taking Darrow to his trial."

Smacking him again, Maribeth wrestled with Clint for a little while. She gave him hell for teasing her and tried several times to pin him down so she could do some teasing of her own. They tired out fairly quickly and when they came to a rest, Maribeth was still on top of him, straddling Clint's waist and breathing heavily after all their exercise.

"You do what you think is right," she said after tossing her hair back with a turn of her head. "And whatever you do, don't let anything that cold-blooded killer has to say get to you. He's trying to get something over on you and don't you forget it."

"I know what he's trying to do. It's just that Darrow isn't the type of man you run into very often, and he can get under your skin if he gets half a chance. Besides, I don't think he's the only one trying to get something over on me."

Maribeth grinned and shifted her weight on top of Clint. "Really, now? And who else might you be talking about?"

Reaching up to take hold of her hips, Clint rubbed her full curves and felt his body responding to her being so close. "I think you might be trying to take advantage of a man that just needs to get some rest before a hard day's work in the morning."

Reaching down to gently rub Clint's hardening penis, she used her other hand to pull up the bottom of her nightgown so that her bare skin was sliding against his. "Taking advantage? Why would I need to do that after you nearly attack me whenever we get alone for a minute?"

Trying to keep the pleasure he felt from showing on his face, Clint let out a deep breath and said, "Maybe that's why I'm not thinking straight. You ever think of that? Maybe your feminine wiles are keeping me from working properly."

"Either that, or you just haven't had enough of me to

keep you satisfied." Feeling that he was fully erect, Maribeth lifted herself up a bit and guided him between her legs. "You ever think of that?"

Clint felt the warm, moist embrace of Maribeth's body taking him inside of her. He slid all the way in as she lowered herself down onto him. Her hands moved slowly over his chest and she leaned her head back while beginning to slowly rock back and forth.

Reaching up to cup her breasts, Clint pressed his head back into the pillow and massaged her smooth, rounded curves. Already, the rest of the night was starting to melt away and all that seemed to matter was what he was doing at that exact moment.

The quiet room became filled with the sound of Maribeth's breathing, which got deeper and faster as she handed herself over to her desires.

"You know something?" Clint said as he pushed up inside of her. "I think I like your theory a lot better than mine."

THIRTY-NINE

She made love to him slowly and with a passion that built up with every passing second. It had started out as gentle and calm, but soon their passion had created a storm that swept them both up into its arms. Maribeth clenched her eyes shut and strained every muscle in her body while riding on top of Clint. She clawed his chest and shoulders while arching her back as she took him inside.

Clint moved his hands over her body, taking hold of her hips and sides, guiding her movements with his hands or the way he moved beneath her. When they found just the right spot, Clint reached down and grabbed her buttocks, pulling her to him again and again as he thrust upward between her legs.

As their pace quickened, Maribeth started to moan. Her voice was soft at first and could only be heard when Clint had pushed as deep inside of her as he could go. Then, as her body became more sensitive, she started groaning louder and for longer periods of time. Finally, as she got herself to bounce up and down on top of him in just the right way, she reached up and slid her fingers through her hair, straightening her back as she began to climax.

Clint could feel her tightening around the base of his

cock. When her body started to tremble, he tightened his grip on her and pumped up into her with powerful motions of his hips. Her legs clamped tightly around his waist and her voice became choked in the back of her throat.

For a moment, it seemed as though she couldn't have moved even if she wanted to. Her back was straight as a board and her head was tossed all the way back. Even her arms were locked in place with her hands buried amid the thick mass of her hair.

Finally, Clint could feel her struggling to take a breath. She shook once and then again before she was able to let out a deep, prolonged gasp. He watched as her eyes opened and she looked down at him. Judging by the tenseness he could still feel in her body, Clint knew that she was still feeling her pleasure surging throughout her entire body.

Clint took hold of her and slid out from between her legs, lowering her onto the mattress right next to where he'd been lying. Maribeth made little noises as though she was just waking up and reached up to touch his stomach as he moved her legs apart and positioned himself between them.

Her pussy was slick and warm and when he slid his cock between the delicate lips, Clint felt Maribeth pull in a quick, excited breath. She started squirming on the bed while he glided in and out, her legs wrapping around him and locking at the ankles.

Clint slid his hands beneath her, lifting her up off the mattress just enough so he could move her lower body the way he wanted. As he moved into her, he pulled her to him, taking complete control of her body while making love to her.

Reaching up with both hands, Maribeth ran her fingers through her hair the way she'd been doing the entire time. It seemed to be her way of surrendering to him, allowing him to have her body and savoring every last second of it. Her eyes were still shut tightly and her lips parted with a silent moan. Pulling in a breath, her back arched again and her breasts were thrust up.

From where he was, Clint got a delicious view of Maribeth's body. The slope of her stomach led down to the warm patch of hair between her legs and led up to the generous mounds of her breasts, topped by large erect nipples. Just looking at her made Clint harder and when he thrust into her again, Maribeth let out the scream that had been building up the entire time.

All Clint had to do was allow himself to focus on nothing but the feeling of being inside of her and the sight of Maribeth's body laid out in front of him and the pleasure started to build up inside. It started as a shortness of breath and once he gave into it, the intensity of his pleasure began to build.

He pumped into her harder and harder. The sound of Maribeth's voice was growing again as she opened her eyes and looked at him with naked desire. She started to reach up to touch him, but soon her breath caught in her throat and the sounds she was making suddenly stopped. Another orgasm was building inside of her. Clint could feel it in the dancer's muscles.

Allowing himself to be consumed by his own pleasure, Clint lowered himself down so that his face was directly over hers. His hips thrust between her legs, driving them both to a powerful climax.

It took a moment or two, but Clint gathered up the strength to move himself over and onto the mattress next to Maribeth. They both lay there for a few minutes before they both eased under the sheets. The instant his head hit the pillow, Clint felt himself start to drift off. He smiled as he heard the muted noises of the saloon beneath the bedroom and he smiled even wider when he thought about

Marvin the barkeep rolling his eyes at the noises coming from above.

Clint thought that Maribeth might have already been asleep, but soon her hands started moving over his chest, tracing widening circles over the front of his body. Lying there, feeling the last traces of their lovemaking working their way beneath his skin, Clint wanted nothing more than to put the rest of the world out of his mind.

Of course, like any forbidden thought, the moment Clint tried to avoid it, that annoying thought popped right back into his mind. He began thinking about the next day and the ride to Winston. He started thinking about the killer in the jailhouse of Broken Cross. He even thought about the killer lying inside of himself.

As if sensing those thoughts, Maribeth nestled her head against his shoulder and whispered, "Just let yourself get some rest, Clint. I can feel you starting to tense up again."

"I was just thinking about—"

"If you want to think about something, think about breakfast. Or you can think about what I've got planned to work up your appetite right before breakfast."

Her hand slid along his body, wandering freely above and below Clint's waist. In no time at all, he was relaxed enough to let sleep carry him through to the dawn.

FORTY

The jailhouse might have been one of the newest buildings in town, but that didn't make it one of the nicest. As far as accommodations went, there was more than a little to be desired. The chill wind blew in through barred windows and even made the bricks of the wall and floor colder to the touch.

That same wind caused a shrill cry whenever it blew at just the right angle. Whenever one of the deputies got up to move around, their footsteps echoed down the hall. Every last cough or clearing of a throat was amplified until it became a roar. And if all those noises weren't enough, the fat man in the cell several doors down from Ellis Darrow would not stop crying.

Jasper had started off whining about how he didn't belong in the cell and how he wasn't about to go anywhere if they'd just let him sleep in his own bed. He begged for another blanket or a visit from his aunt who lived just outside of town. After that he'd gone back to crying and since then he'd been whining like a little dog chasing rabbits in its sleep.

Ellis Darrow sat on his bunk with his feet kicked up and his hand folded behind his head. The pillow on his cot wasn't more than a bag of rags and the mattress wasn't thick enough to keep the splinters from wedging into his back. But the music of the jailhouse was more than enough to ease his mind.

The deputies outside his cell wouldn't take their eyes off of him, which had made it uncomfortable at first. Pacing back and forth, making their ignorant comments, the younger lawmen had been doing a good job of making sure Darrow didn't get a wink of sleep. Of course, they'd been hoping to scare the killer with their threats of violence, but the only thing that had gotten on Darrow's nerves was the sound of their voices.

It was so much easier for him to bear once Darrow concentrated on the more restful noises drifting through the jail. Namely, Jasper's crying provided Darrow not only with amusement but serenity as well. It did him good to hear the fat man's suffering. That was an indication that at least something had gone right during the eventful evening.

Footsteps clattered down the hall, leading away from Darrow's cell. Soon, there came the clatter of a cell door being rattled on its hinges.

"Shut the hell up, Jasper," one of the deputies said.

After one last whine, Jasper choked back his suffering until it sounded as though he'd been smothered by a pillow. Darrow opened one of his eyes a crack and saw that it was the bigger of the two deputies that had made the trip down the hall to rattle the fat man's cage. Typical. Darrow shook his head slightly and readjusted his position on the cot. If he couldn't listen to Jasper's crying, he would have to find some other way to ease himself into sleep. After all, tomorrow was going to be another big day in his life.

The instant he moved, Darrow heard the deputy outside his cell tap something against the bars of his door.

"Hey," the lawman whispered. "I saw you moving in there. I know you're not sleepin'."

Darrow opened his eyes and looked at the deputy.

Seeing that he had the killer's attention, the deputy made sure it was obvious he'd used the barrel of his gun to tap against the bars. "You see this?" he asked, lifting his gun into the dim light of the closest lantern. "This is the same gun I'll use to blow your brains out if you say one word."

Darrow kept looking at the deputy. His face didn't so much as twitch.

"That's right, you son of a bitch. You're such a bad man when you're heeled and now you ain't nothing. Tell you what . . ." The deputy got up and stood in front of the cell. The other lawman must have taken notice, because the one Darrow could see waved down the hall and said, "It's all right. I know what I'm doing. Just stay down there and tell me if you see anyone coming."

There was a moment of silence and then a series of footsteps which dwindled away until they stopped.

Darrow could picture that bigger deputy standing at the front door, craning his neck so he could watch the pathetic little show taking place in the back of the jailhouse.

Turning his attention to Darrow, the remaining deputy reached across his belly with his left hand and lifted the keys that were hanging from his belt. He dangled them in the air like a strip of meat in front of a dog before inserting one key into the lock and turning it.

There was a metallic *clank* and then the door swung open an inch or so outward. "There," the deputy said. "The door's open. Why don't you try to get out now?"

When Darrow sat up and dropped his feet to the floor, he saw the deputy tense up. The killer rose slowly to his feet, but didn't walk forward. All the while, he studied the look on the deputy's face. There was no doubting the fact that the lawman was scared. But there was also no doubting that he would use his gun if he got the chance.

If he got the chance.

"That's it, asshole," the deputy said as a nervous smile came onto his nodding face. "Come on and try to step through this door. Give me a reason to make you pay for the blood you spilled."

Darrow took one step as though he was trying to walk through a vat of molasses. The next two steps he took were so quick that the deputy barely even had time to react to them before the killer was at the door and reaching through it with one hand.

It was sheer reflex and nerves that were already almost ready to snap that got the deputy's gun pointed in the right direction. Its barrel touched the killer's stomach and he didn't do a damn thing about it until the hammer was just about to fall. Then, only as an afterthought, Darrow batted the weapon out of the deputy's hand.

Footsteps were charging down the hall by now and the bigger deputy was shouting something to his partner, but Darrow wasn't paying any attention to that. Instead, he was more intent on the look on the smaller deputy's face and the stench of fear that surrounded him like the stink of shit in a barnyard.

"You want to talk tough, you'd best know who you're talking to first, boy," Darrow snarled. "And if you want to kill me, then you'd best just shoot me through these bars because I'm not about to let you be the hero tonight."

With that, Darrow took a step back and pulled the jail door shut. Just as the door clanged against its jamb, the bigger deputy charged forward and shoved his gun into Darrow's face. The blunt end of the barrel knocked against his mouth, chipping one of Darrow's front teeth.

"Get back into that cell, you piece of shit," the deputy said while his partner staggered back away from the door. Without taking his eyes away from his prisoner, the deputy asked his partner, "Are you all right?" He didn't get an answer right away, so he repeated the question.

The shorter of the two lawmen scrambled to push the fear off his face and just barely managed to do so before his partner took a quick look at him. "I'm fine," he said after retrieving his pistol. "Just lock that bastard up and leave me alone."

Twisting the key in the lock, the bigger deputy secured the door to the jail cell and sat back down on the stool where he'd been perched for the better part of the night. Darrow had backed off a couple steps to keep out of the deputy's reach, but kept his eyes locked on the man who'd been taunting him only moments before.

The smaller deputy did his best to return the killer's gaze, but found himself looking away after a couple tense seconds. He simply hadn't expected the prisoner to move so fast when a gun was pointed directly at him. The fact that Darrow didn't seem to care if he was charging into a bullet rattled the deputy down to his core.

It wasn't often that a man came across someone with so much disrespect for life, even his own. The clearest thing that the deputy recalled was the look in Darrow's eyes.

That killer had wanted to prove that he could get to anyone at any time, even if it meant risking his own hide to do it. Not only had the point been made, but it gave the deputy something to think about for the rest of the entire night. He was certain that if Darrow was given even a fraction of a chance, he would be able to walk out of that jailhouse, leaving behind yet another pile of bodies in his wake.

Suddenly, the deputy wasn't thinking about killing Ellis Darrow. He was thinking about how a man like that could be killed at all. The murderer looked like a walking corpse already, and he didn't have a fearful bone in his body. He didn't listen to reason and he couldn't be dealt with. The only thing that seemed to matter to him was whatever twisted desires went through his own mind.

Ellis Darrow wasn't just some mad dog.

He was the stuff nightmares were made of. He was a monster.

"You all right?" the bigger deputy asked his partner.

Shaking himself out of his thoughts, the lawman replied, "Yeah. I'm fine."

"Well we'd best keep awake until dawn. That's when this here bastard is gonna be dragged out of here so he can stand trial."

"Good. Just so long as he gets away from here. Far away."

FORTY-ONE

Clint couldn't remember the last time he'd had such a good night's sleep. Perhaps it was the fact that the day before had been so long and so terrible that anything else would seem like heaven in comparison. Then again, it could have also been because of the way he'd started the brand-new day.

Even before his eyes had opened, Clint felt Maribeth's lips grazing the naked skin of his stomach. He could feel her rustling beneath the sheets and soon she was placing gentle kisses down his abdomen, making her way between his legs. His body was already responding to her and by the time she'd taken his penis all the way inside her mouth, he was fully erect.

She sucked on him hungrily until he was about to explode inside her mouth. From there, he moved her back up onto the mattress so he could settle between her legs and slide inside of her. They made love as the sun came up and when they were finished, Clint felt alive and completely refreshed.

"Damn," he said while pulling on his clothes. "The Tweed House really does have some of the best service in town. I'd even venture to say the entire state."

Maribeth was slipping into a clean dress that was the color of faded roses. Tying her hair into a single tail which fell over her right shoulder, she said, "If you say that I must give this same treatment to anyone who sleeps here, I'll smack the taste out of your mouth."

Clint held up his hands as if surrendering and let her push him roughly aside while making her way to the door. "I'm only kidding," he said. "You know that." Before she walked past him, he grabbed her around the waist and pulled her close. "Come here. I want to thank you for all you've done."

"It wasn't much. Just a bed and some free food."

"But you were there and you cared for me. That means a lot. Thanks, Maribeth." With that, Clint leaned in and kissed her on the lips. It was soft and gentle at first, but the passion grew until they forced themselves to break contact.

"No need to thank me, Clint. You came through for me in a big way and I know you'd do it again. You're a good man and don't forget it. No matter what any other crazy, evil men out there say to you, don't ever forget you're a good man."

Clint looked into her eyes and instantly knew that she meant every word she'd said with every fiber in her being. Seeing such earnestness in her face gave him a genuine boost of strength. He could feel her confidence in him like cement to fill in the cracks of a wall.

He wanted to tell her how he felt. He wanted to at least thank her again, but Clint found that no words were necessary. Instead, they embraced for a couple seconds and let their feelings be felt by the other. It must have worked just as well for both of them because when they finally took a step away from each other, they were both smiling widely.

"All right," Maribeth said. "Enough of all of this. I need to get you downstairs before your breakfast gets cold."

"You really didn't have to go through all of this."

"Well you should've told me that last night, because that's when I arranged for it. And don't be too grateful just yet. I couldn't get the cook at Jesse's in time, so I had to have the cook here at the saloon make something for you. I just hope it doesn't sit in your stomach and weigh you down when you ride to Winston."

They joked some more back and forth while heading downstairs to the main room of the saloon. There weren't half as many people inside the place, but several of the tables were still occupied and the piano player was filling the air with a steady flow of upbeat music.

As soon as they walked up to the bar, one of the server girls caught their attention and directed them to a table not too far from the empty stage. The breakfast she brought out to them was hot, but it reminded Clint of an old joke about a man getting served a meal in prison. The bad news was that all there was to eat was horse shit. The good news was that there was plenty of it.

The runny eggs, mushy potatoes and crisp bacon weren't exactly horse shit, but it was bad enough to remind Clint of that particular comparison. The good news, however, was that there was plenty of it. Clint was so hungry that once he got used to the taste, he was happy just to fill his stomach. The coffee was strong enough to wash it all down anyway.

"So will you be all right after this passes?" Clint asked, crunching on a bit of bacon that didn't seem to want to be chewed.

"I'm all right now."

"I mean with Jasper trying to clean you out and everything. You're out a partner, after all."

Maribeth waved away the question like a fly buzzing around her head. "Jasper trying to turn on me was a surprise and it could have been bad. Jasper getting caught and sent to jail, on the other hand, is the best thing that could've happened to me. I needed his backing before, but now that I'm established, I'll do just fine on my own once his shares are signed over to me. I know a few lawyers in town and they should be more than happy to work on a case involving that much money. At least I don't have to listen to his whining every day."

"I'm glad to hear it. You really deserve all your success. You've worked hard enough and waited long enough for it."

Lifting her cup of coffee, Maribeth said, "I'll drink to that."

They finished their breakfast without talking about Jasper or Darrow again. Instead, they caught up on old times and swapped stories the way they would have done if none of the business at the bank had ever happened. It felt good for Clint to lose himself in such idle chatter. That way, he felt all the more rested once it was time to get going.

Taking his hand in hers, Maribeth walked with Clint out of The Tweed House and all the way to the livery. She watched as Clint saddled Eclipse and loaded the saddle bags onto the Darley Arabian's back.

"I need to collect Darrow and head out," Clint said.

Nodding, Maribeth gave him one more hug and kissed him on the cheek. "Be careful," she said one last time.

Clint nodded, paid the stable boy for Eclipse's stall and headed for the sheriff's office.

FORTY-TWO

Sheriff Anderson as well as all of his remaining deputies were on hand to watch as Clint came by to take custody of Ellis Darrow. The lawmen said hardly a sentence among them as the prisoner was dragged from his cell in shackles, lifted onto an old, rundown mule and tied to the saddle.

Anderson walked up to Clint and handed him a small key ring. "These are for the chains," the sheriff said. "And that old nag he's riding couldn't run if its life depended on it. It should keep up a solid pace so you could still ride through the night if you had to, but as far as him making a break for it—"

"Don't worry about that," Clint said while shaking his head. "He won't."

"I've been thinking. If you want someone to come with you, I can spare a man or two."

"Second thoughts, Sheriff?"

"Not about you, but about him," Anderson said, nodding over toward Darrow who was chained down to the mule's back. "He damn near got out again last night."

"But he didn't."

"No."

174

"So that's what matters. What about the woman?"

At the very mention of that subject, Anderson twisted up his face as though he'd just tasted something awful. "She's locked up in the old cells in the back of my office. She's been crying to get a look at him all night, but I won't have none of it. She can see him all she wants after they both swing."

Clint nodded. He'd been hoping that the sheriff would know better than to let Ann anywhere near Darrow throughout the night. He didn't care how many deputies were watching them, Clint would have had to assume that Darrow was armed if that woman of his had gotten her hands anywhere near him.

All Clint had to do was look at the looks on all the lawmen's faces to know that they'd spent a sleepless night looking over all the prisoners. Not only did the sheriff and deputies look on edge and glad to be rid of Darrow, but they all seemed downright spooked.

"You watch yourself," Anderson said once Clint had taken hold of the mule's reins. "This one's full of surprises and he's got nothin' in this world to lose. That makes him the worst kind of dangerous."

"I know that, Sheriff. Thanks for the warning all the same."

Anderson tipped his hat and took a step back. He and the deputies watched Clint start heading for the edge of town. The solemn looks on their faces reminded Clint of a funeral. Being sure to keep the mule slightly ahead of Eclipse, Clint returned the sheriff's final wave and set his sights to the road ahead.

The entire town was quiet as a tomb. It seemed as though every single face that lived there was peeking through a window, looking around a corner, or staring at them from the side of the street. Every single one of them looked just as spooked as the lawmen and not one of them was unhappy to watch them go.

Wanting to conserve Eclipse's and the mule's energy, Clint left town at a leisurely pace. He also did so to let the intense stares of all the locals get a chance to burn into Darrow's hide. Since he could feel the hatred coming off the townspeople, Clint figured Darrow must have been burning up under their scrutiny.

If the killer did feel any of it, however, he didn't give the first sign. His hands were chained behind his back and his feet were connected to the mule by another chain, which was locked to his ankles and ran under the mule's belly. He slouched in the saddle, rocking with the pack animal's movements and shuddering as his body was wracked by a series of violent coughing fits.

Every so often, Darrow would clear his throat and send a juicy wad of bloody spit from his mouth and onto the ground. Besides the sound of the horses' hooves plodding into the dirt and Darrow's spitting, the only other sound that could be heard was the screaming coming from the old jail cells.

"I want to see him!" Ann screamed through the cracks in the walls and the holes in the ceiling. "I need to see him! You've got to let me see him!"

Once they'd ridden out of Broken Cross, Clint and Darrow picked up the pace, heading for the wide open, barren stretch of trail leading to the town of Winston.

"I'll be seeing you, darlin'," Darrow said in a hoarse whisper. "I'll see you soon enough."

FORTY-THREE

Darrow waited until Broken Cross was nothing more than a memory left far behind them. The sun was cresting in the sky, but the air was still crisp and cool as a wind blew over the flatlands. It was one of those days that would be gray from sunrise to sunset, without a drop of rain ever falling. The clouds were too high up and too thin to worry about rain. Even an inexperienced trailsman would know that much.

Since the sun was all but hidden in the overcast sky, all the colors around the pair of riders seemed washed out as well. The branches of the trees, already losing their leafy covers, seemed especially stark and barren. The color of the bark was more like that of an old hide that had been stretched out and forgotten on the side of an abandoned barn.

The mule was starting to wheeze almost as much as the prisoner on its back. Clint kept an eye on the broken-down animal, but was certain the mule would be plenty strong enough to make the trip. It wouldn't be going anywhere else once it reached Winston, but he was certain Sheriff Anderson knew that when he'd handed Clint the reins.

Even though the animal was tough, the killer on top of

him seemed to have even more stamina than Clint and both animals combined. No matter how much he coughed or how much blood was kicked up from his lungs, Darrow simply refused to fall over in the saddle. He kept his head up and his eyes focused on Clint.

Once noon had passed, Darrow's crimson-stained lips parted to let out something besides a hacking cough. "You been thinking about what I said?" the killer asked. "You been thinking about how this is all gonna end between you and me?"

Without turning to look at the prisoner head-on, Clint said, "We're not married, Darrow. There is no 'you and me.'"

The killer stretched his back and rolled his shoulders to help loosen his muscles. His shuddering cough soon took on a different rhythm and before long, it became clear that he was laughing. "We might as well be married, Adams. You know . . . till death do us part and all of that."

Clint shook his head. "For someone who travels with a lady as pretty as the one you left in a cell back there, I would've thought you'd want to think more about her instead of me. I guess I didn't picture you as one of those types."

After spitting a mouthful of blood to one side, Darrow said, "You know what I mean, Adams. The only time we're parting ways is when one of us is dead. You know it and I know it. And if you think about it long enough, I'll bet you'd agree that both of us won't even make it to Winston."

"Is that so?"

"Yeah," Darrow said with a nod that looked more like his neck had lost the strength to hold his head up. "That's so."

Clint looked around and saw that they were on a stretch of trail that cut through a field as flat as a tabletop with only an occasional rock or clump of trees to break the monotony. Even the trees seemed lonely since there wasn't a group of them with more than three or four trunks in the lot. He pulled back on Eclipse's reins, which also brought Darrow's mule to a stop.

Without saying a word, Clint swung down from his saddle and dropped to the ground. He fished in his pocket for the keys Sheriff Anderson gave him and walked toward the wheezing mule.

"What's this, Adams? You coming to your senses and letting me go before you get hurt?" Darrow's grin displayed a set of chipped teeth coated with blood. His breath smelled like a slaughterhouse and he was sweating as though he'd been forced to run all the way out of Broken Cross.

Clint circled the mule, stopping to bend at the knees and unlock the shackles around Darrow's ankles. From there, he took the killer's elbow and yanked him down from the saddle. Darrow landed on his feet, but needed Clint's help to keep his balance.

"Now you got me curious," Darrow said. The amusement had drained from his voice as he watched with weary eyes as Clint unlocked the cuffs around his wrists. He rubbed the chafed skin where the handcuffs had been and swallowed a bloody wad of saliva. "I asked you a question, Adams. What's going on here?"

Clint stood directly in front of the killer and stared him directly in the eyes. "You say you know me. You say you know what kind of man I am? Well I know you just as well. Maybe even better. You're not just sick. You're dying, and there's nothing any doctor can do for you. Or at least, there's nothing you're willing to let anyone do for you."

"Oh, you figured all that out all by yourself?" Darrow said. His skin was the color of bleached bone and his lips were light blue. His eyes, however, were clear as crystal and they burned with a fire all their own. "So you got eyes and ears. So what?"

"That's not all I know about you, Darrow. I know that since you can feel yourself dying a little more each day, you've given yourself over to it. You've made a pact with God or the devil or whoever would listen that you wouldn't let yourself waste away. You would die on your own terms since that would be the only way you could beat the sickness that's chewing you up heart, body and soul."

A good deal of the smugness was gone from Darrow's face. The fire was still in his eyes, but the smile wasn't anywhere to be found upon his bloody lips.

"You decided this life because you saw it as a quick, exciting road to the grave," Clint went on. "But once you took up your gun, you discovered one small hitch in your plans. You found out the hard way that since you've got nothing to lose, you're not the type to pause when things look dangerous. And since you've already stared death in the face, you don't hesitate when the lead starts to fly.

"Threats don't mean a damn thing to you since there's nothing anyone can say that's worse than the hand you've already been dealt. The ironic part is because of all of that, you tend to come out on top of all the situations that should have killed you."

Darrow nodded slowly. "Sounds like you've got a good handle on things after all. So why let me go?"

"I'm not letting you go." Clint took two steps back, drew his Colt and said, "I'm calling your bluff."

FORTY-FOUR

Darrow put on a smile that was every bit as disturbing as it was annoying. His eyes flared with a scalding fire and he rubbed his hands vigorously together. "Now the Gunsmith shows his true colors. The great man himself has to take me out to the middle of nowhere so he can look like the hero when he drags my carcass to town. Go on then, hero. Do your worst."

Lifting the Colt up so he could stare down its barrel, Clint aimed for a second and then turned the pistol over and released the cylinder. One by one, the shells dropped out of the gun until there was only one remaining. After lining up the single bullet in the chamber, Clint snapped the cylinder shut and tossed the gun to the ground between himself and Darrow.

"I'm not an executioner," Clint said. "But I am proving a point."

Nodding, Darrow held his hands apart and loosened his fingers. Every muscle in his body tensed, making him look like a snake that was preparing to strike.

Clint stood still as a statue. His hands hung loosely at his sides and his hips were cocked at a casual angle. When Darrow snapped forward in a sudden burst of motion,

Clint hardly even responded. In fact, he waited until the killer's hands closed around the Colt before taking a step forward.

It wasn't even a quick step. Just a movement to close some of the distance between them.

With a victorious smile, Darrow straightened up and held the gun pointing at Clint. "Now this is what I call ironic. The big hero getting shot with his own weapon. The Gunsmith dropped by a man on his last legs. I guess not being afraid of death really does give me an edge."

The Colt was close enough for Clint to catch a whiff of the oil he'd used to clean it last. He stared down the gun's barrel as though he was looking into the black eye of death itself and he didn't even come close to blinking.

After a moment, Clint shook his head once and said, "That's where you're wrong. It took me a while to figure it out, but I eventually realized what kind of man you truly are."

"Yeah, yeah. We already went all through that speech."

"Actually, I never finished it. You see, you make yourself look like the man knocking on death's door with nothing to lose. You play the part real well and scare a lot of people while hurting a lot more. But like anyone playing the cards you've been dealt, your actions give away what's really going on inside your head.

"Some men twitch when they bluff or scratch their nose when they get a good hand. You step aside at the last second when you could have gotten yourself killed for sure."

Darrow's brow furrowed, but the gun didn't waver a bit. "What are you talking about?"

"In the bank, when I had that same gun on you, a man with a real death wish would have gone out in his blaze of glory. But not you. Instead, you gave yourself up and went along quietly with the law. And from what I hear about that break you could have made from jail, you should have been out of there and halfway to the border by now. But instead, you hung around until I got there.

"You could have at least shot Jasper. That's what really tipped me off about you. Anyone who didn't give a damn about life would have surely blown that fat man to hell when he had his chance. You could have gotten a few shots off at me or some of the deputies in the fight and gone out in an even bigger blaze of glory. But you didn't. Did you?"

Clint's words were starting to get under Darrow's skin. His pale lips were pressed together and his knuckles were turning even whiter around the modified Colt in his grip. "That was my choice, Adams. All of them were my choices. I'll die my way. My way!"

"You're no better than anyone else," Clint said. "You got a bad deal with being so sick, but you're still afraid of death. I could see that in your eyes at the last second. I didn't recognize it until I thought it over, but the fear was there. It's still there. I can see it right now."

"Shut up. I'll kill you."

"Why? Why kill me if you want to die so damn bad?"

"I thought you might be the one," Darrow said in a voice that was more of a hiss. "I thought you could be the one to kill me. Not some deputy and not that asshole sheriff. I wanted you to do it. And I wanted to go on my own terms.

"I thought you were going to shoot me down at the bank, but you stopped. I thought you were going to do it in the jailhouse once you got a look at those deputies I killed, but you didn't. You know what I think? You might have lost your nerve, Adams. You might just be getting old and soft."

Clint stared into Darrow's eyes for a second before his hand snapped up and took hold of the Colt. The motion was faster than Darrow's eyes could have possibly seen and by the time the killer knew what was going on, Clint was already twisting the Colt away from him.

In the next second, Clint brought his hand up and pressed the end of the barrel against Darrow's forehead.

"Go on." Darrow wheezed. Suddenly his strength seemed to have left him and his voice was trembling and weak. "Go on and do it. I can tell you want to."

"And I know why you want me to. Getting shot like this would end it all quickly, wouldn't it? Just a sharp pain and then nothing after that. Isn't that what you've heard? And rather than try to shoot yourself or take your chances with some cowboy at a saloon somewhere when you can go against someone who knows how to handle a gun? You were waiting for a chance like this weren't you? Waiting to go against someone like me.

"I could make it quick and painless. I could end it all with one shot, guaranteed. And in the bargain, you get to die with your name attached to mine so that maybe someone will remember who the hell you were."

Suddenly, Clint's other hand snapped up and clamped around Darrow's throat. Easing the Colt back into its holster, Clint stared into the other man's face and started to squeeze. "You want to die so bad? Let me hear you ask for it. Let me hear you beg for it, tough man." As he spoke, all of the rage he'd been holding back since he first laid eyes on the corpses in that bank and in the jailhouse started bubbling to the surface. Every moment he'd let pass because it wasn't the right one had been leading up to this. Every opportunity Clint had had to act had lead him here.

Darrow's face turned even paler than it had been and he reached up to grab hold of Clint's arm. Even though he tried to pull himself free, Darrow was just too weak. His body simply wouldn't let him get away.

"This is it, Darrow," Clint said. "This is what you wanted. Only you don't get to have it quick and painless. You get to feel the terror and pain that went through the minds of all those folks you killed. But what's more important is that you get to come to grips with who you really are. You're a sick, frightened man who didn't even have the courage to die with dignity."

After trying one last time to pull himself free, Darrow let one hand hang from Clint's arm by his fingertips. The rest of him dangled at the end of Clint's fist like a dead fish on a hook.

"You're not getting the quick way out, Darrow. If anyone's earned the hard road to hell, it's you. You were wrong about yourself and you were also wrong about me." With that, Clint relaxed his grip and let Darrow drop to the ground. "I'm not a killer. The only killer here is you. And killers stand trial. After that, they hang."

Darrow's head dropped forward and his entire body seemed to shrivel at the thought of having the air choked out of him again.

Clint didn't have to see the other man's eyes to know what he would find.

Fear.

Clint took hold of Darrow and forced him back onto the mule's back. The killer didn't struggle at all when Clint put the chains back on him and he didn't say another word for the rest of the ride to Winston. He stood trial and he made it all the way to the gallows, the only sound he made being the coughs, which tore him apart from the inside out.

Clint didn't stay to watch the hanging. He rode out of town, knowing that he'd done his part. Darrow might not have lived too much longer than that day on the trail, but he lived long enough to regret what he'd done. In that regret, there was justice.

Justice came for Ann DiGrasse as well. Sheriff Anderson saw to that.

Watch for

FACES OF THE DEAD

260th novel in the exciting GUNSMITH series
from Jove

Coming in August!

**Explore the exciting Old West with one
of the men who made it wild!**